THE BIG PICTURE

THE BIG PICTURE

FINDING THE SPIRITUAL MESSAGE IN MOVIES

J. John & Mark Stibbe

Authentic

07 06 05 04 03 02 7 6 5 4 3 2 1

First published 2002 by Authentic Lifestyle, an imprint of
Authentic Media, 9 Holdom Avenue, Bletchley, Milton Keynes, Bucks,
MK1 1QR, UK.

Distributed in the USA by Gabriel Resources,
P.O. Box 1047, Waynesboro, GA 30830-2047, USA

British Library Cataloguing in Publication Data
A catalogue record for this book is available from the British Library

ISBN 1-86024-279-0

Cover design by David Lund
Printed in Great Britain by
Bell & Bain Ltd., Glasgow

Contents

INTRODUCTION

There are few things we enjoy more than watching a movie, either at the cinema, or at home. Movies have an amazing ability to move us when other forms of communication leave us untouched.

Recently, we had a funeral at our church for a 24-year-old called Stefan, who died in a motorbike accident. Stef's mother and father had watched the movie, *Captain Corelli's Mandolin* and had fallen in love with the Greek island featured on the film. They had visited the island for a holiday just a few months before their son's death. One evening, sitting together in the fading sun, they started to discuss the terrible suffering visited on that island during the German occupation. One thing led to another and they began to consider how they would cope if they lost one of their three sons. They concluded that they would only be able to get through such a loss by the grace of God. Shortly after this, their eldest son was tragically killed, and they asked us to play the main theme tune from *Captain Corelli* over and over in the thirty minutes before the funeral. I doubt whether anyone was left unmoved by the poignant sounds of this musical theme.

The fact is, films have an extraordinary power to communicate spiritually, not just emotionally. Recently, a girl in her twenties said that she had sensed God speaking to her during the science fiction film, *Gattaca*. The example of one of the characters in the movie had inspired her to believe that she too could fulfil her potential and become the person God had created her to be. She said that since that day she had not looked back, and that she had discovered a new desire to persevere.

It is our belief that God exists and that he speaks to people today. He doesn't just speak through the Bible in church buildings on Sunday mornings (though he certainly does that). He also speaks through the movies in the cinema during the week. Neither of us believes for one moment that God only lives and works in sacred buildings. He is far bigger and greater than that. He can as easily speak through a movie director like Steven Spielberg as he can through a church leader like the Archbishop of Canterbury. God is not confined to the obviously religious contexts. He speaks through poetry, stories, pictures, films, television shows, and through every creative art form and every kind of mass media communication. If we are prepared to think outside the box, we will encounter the Creator God in the multicoloured world of human creativity.

In this book, we look at eight films that have, in some way or other, transmitted a spiritual message that has made an impact on us. Some of these films contain adult content that, on its own, would be morally questionable, but which, within the film concerned fulfils a vital function in the plot. Yet, even in the midst of the mediocre and even the dark, we have found a ray of spiritual light to stimulate, enrich and illuminate. As J.R.R. Tolkien once wrote, 'We have come from God, and inevitably the myths woven by us, though they contain error, will also reflect a splintered fragment of the true light, the eternal truth that is with God.'

While several of our films contain violence (*The Godfather*, *Saving Private Ryan* and *Fargo*), they have still proven to be a vehicle through which God has spoken.

We believe that filmmakers are today's mythmakers. Contemporary films tell the stories that reflect the spiritual longings of our post-modern world. In the light of that, we believe it is important to keep in touch with popular culture, particularly as it is reflected in the cinema. We are both committed to a spirituality that is relevant to everyday life. Jesus communicated spiritual truths through down-to-earth stories called parables. Many modern movies are like parables. They tell stories that have transcendent resonance. They are like windows onto the landscape of modern spirituality.

At the same time, neither of us is uncritical about the films we choose to see. As Christians, we believe that we need to be discerning and wise about what we view, both at home and at the cinema. The Apostle Paul wrote, 'Live as children of light (for the fruit of the light consists in all goodness, righteousness and truth) and find out what pleases the Lord. Have nothing to do with the fruitless deeds of darkness, but rather expose them' (Ephesians 5.8–11).

We are therefore careful not to see films that are blasphemous, sexually explicit, gratuitously violent and overtly occult in content. The Bible very clearly encourages us to avoid such things and to think about what is noble, excellent and pure. At the same time, we don't believe that we are to live our lives hidden within the walls of a church, never watching television, never going to the movies, never connecting with our culture. Indeed, we are not alone today in comparing the messages we have found in movies to the teachings of the Bible.

In the final analysis, we want to encourage a kind of two-level approach to films. At one level, just enjoy the movie, listening to the dialogue and watching the action purely at the level of entertainment. At the same time, be aware of the deeper levels that can sometimes exist in a film. Many of these may be unintended by the author of the screenplay or the director of the film. Yet, God is bigger than the intentions of those involved in the production, direction and editing of a film. He can speak in ways unintended by human beings. He can address us morally and spiritually through a film, challenging us, comforting us, even enlightening us. So, listen and watch at a deeper level too. Be open to hearing God's voice at Warner Brothers, UCI, or wherever. Not every film will achieve this two-level dynamic of communication. Some will prove to be paper thin in terms of meaning and significance. But other films will speak to your soul, not just your senses. Be prepared to be surprised and delighted by the Spirit of God.

Why not pray before you view a movie that you would be receptive to the voice of God while you watch and listen? Here, in conclusion, is a prayer we suggest you might like to pray:

> Dear God,
>
> Thank you so much for the movies, for their power to instruct, to move, to entertain.
>
> Thank you for speaking through films, even when the film-makers haven't intended it.
>
> Thank you for this film I am about to watch.

If there is anything you want to say to me through the words and pictures of this film, please do that. I open my ears to your word and my heart to your love. Speak to me.

If there is anything in this film that you find offensive, please alert me to that and protect me from the images and the values transmitted.

Help me to understand my culture better through this experience. Enable me to see the signs of the times as I watch.

Please let me encounter you so that I may become a better person, a more fulfilled person, a person more like Jesus, the greatest storyteller of all.

In his name,

Amen.

1

The Hand that Pulls the Strings

The Godfather Trilogy

J. John

1972, 1974, 1990, Paramount

Director: Francis Ford Coppola

Starring:
Marlon Brando
Al Pacino
Robert De Niro
Diane Keaton
Robert Duval

Classification: 18

In 1972, a movie was released based on Mario Puzo's novel, *The Godfather*. Thirty years on, Francis Ford Coppola's film maintains its position as one of the most popular and critically acclaimed in cinematic history. It won three Oscars: for best picture, best screenplay and best actor (although Marlon Brando refused to accept the award). *The Godfather*, along with its two sequels, *The Godfather Part II* (1974) and *The Godfather Part III* (1990), form the famous trilogy depicting the life of the Corleone family. It has become such a cultural icon that in the 1998 film *You've Got Mail*, Tom Hanks even suggests that the answers to all life's questions can be found in *The Godfather*.

A Family Within 'the Family'

The Corleones are not just any old family: they are deeply enmeshed in the underworld of organised crime. *The Godfather* is about Mafia Don, Vito Corleone, and the passing of the 'family business' to one of his sons, Michael. This is an insightful study of violence, power and corruption, honour and obligation, justice and crime. In the opening scene of the film, the camera pulls back very slowly from the face of a man in Vito Corleone's office, where he is regally and ruthlessly carrying on his business during his daughter's wedding reception (being held in the compound of his home). In the low-lit office, Corleone is sitting behind his desk, while he lovingly and gently strokes the head of a cat perched on his lap. Although he moves stiffly, Corleone wields enormous, lethal power as he dispenses his own terrifying form of justice, determining who will be punished and who will be favoured.

The Godfather is also a film about family. It begins at a wedding, and *Part I* ends at a baptism. *Part III* ends with the family going to the opera. In between, the action is interspersed with scenes of weddings, funerals, pregnancies, illnesses, family dinners and family feuds.

This is the great paradox of *The Godfather*: on the one hand, it portrays the common life of a family, while on the other it shows the bizarre, sensational, violent life of 'the family' (i.e. the Mafia).

Clip One: The Baptism Scene

Michael Corleone, Vito's son, has agreed to become the godfather to his new nephew. The baptism scene that follows is one of the most memorable in cinematic history. In a beautiful Italian church, Michael and his wife Kay stand holding baby Michael, who is dressed in an ornate Christening gown. As the priest prepares the baby for baptism, he asks Michael a number of questions.

'Do you believe in the Father, the Son and the Holy Ghost?' 'Do you renounce evil?'

'Yes', he replies to each in turn, without batting an eyelid. There is no hint in his face as to what is happening elsewhere. But as the questions are being asked, we cut one by one to the brutal killing of six men, gunned down in cold blood on the orders of Corleone. The organ reaches its dramatic crescendo in the church as, elsewhere the guns fire and blood is spilled. The priest concludes the service with: 'Go in peace, and may the Lord be with you.'

Religion and Reality

It is never enough simply to mouth Christian platitudes. It is not enough to be baptised, married and buried in the Church.

The Christian faith is all about transformed lives. *The Godfather* presents us with extreme examples of hypocrisy, but these all started in small ways somewhere earlier. It should make us ask whether we are riding along the same tracks of hypocrisy that led, ultimately, to the spectacular examples we see in the film.

The easiest person for you to deceive is yourself. There is always a danger that we separate what we say from what we do, which enables us to pretend to be something or someone we are not. So, mouthing religious platitudes does not guarantee us acceptance by Christ, his approval or a ticket to heaven. You might tell the hospital receptionist, for instance, that your religion is 'C of E', but have you ever been along to your local church?

I once asked a man why he didn't go to church, and he replied that he sent his wife along instead 'to keep up the insurance policy'. I pointed out to him the fact that God doesn't issue joint policies. You need to believe in him for yourself.

Being religious does not in itself guarantee a relationship with God. Instead, friendship with God involves humility and honesty. After all, you don't become a saint just by putting on Marks & Spencer underwear.

Who's Pulling Your Strings?

The title scene of the film uses the same image that appears on the original cover of the novel. It depicts an arm reaching downwards, with its hand clasping a wooden crosspiece, to which strings are attached. This symbol points to the theme of both the novel and the film.

In the book, Don Corleone proclaims to the other dons, 'We are all men, who have refused to be fools, who have refused to be puppets dancing on a string, pulled by the men on high.' But what *does* control us? Don't we all, to some degree or other, have strings attached?

Take the past, for example. We can't seem to escape it, and it affects us all. It is no good pretending otherwise. Then there is the issue of genetics: at a biological level, we are all complex chains of DNA, which seem in some way to determine who we are and who we are to become. Of course, it's becoming ever easier to blame our behaviour on our genetic make-up. It's tempting to abdicate responsibility for our actions, suggesting instead that it's the fault of our genes.

You often hear people blaming their present behaviour on the way their parents have brought them up. 'I had a lousy background,' they say. 'I only do what I saw my parents doing. It's too late to change.'

The present also comes with strings attached. In today's environment of global capitalism and market forces, there is enormous pressure to have everything, and to want more. Peer pressure also affects us. Have you ever done something wrong, only to say, 'My mates made me do it'? Force of habit is another good excuse: 'I have always done it; I can't get out of it; I can't break the bonds.' And, of course, there's the small matter of fate, destiny, bad luck or even a curse . . .

Freedom From the Ties that Bind

The strings of both the past and the present can only be broken by Jesus Christ. In the Bible, Psalm 129 states that 'the Lord is good; he has cut the cords used by the ungodly to bind me'. Elsewhere, God tells the prophet Hosea: 'I led them [the people of Israel] with cords of human kindness, with ties of love; I lifted the yoke from their neck and bent down to feed them' (Hosea 11:4).

Can we ever escape our strings? In one sense, no. After all, a puppet without strings is a pile of wood. But we need oversight and guidance, not control.

At the beginning of time, Adam and Eve were tempted to break free from God, and disastrous consequences followed. They put themselves, and us, under the control of someone else, who pulls our strings and makes us dance towards destruction.

God holds the strings to salvation, but he never pulls them for us. He won't force us into anything. He offers us the free gift of salvation through what Jesus has done on the Cross. But he will never compel us to accept that gift. We must choose of our own free will, and we must express that choice by honestly admitting our need of forgiveness.

Clip Two: Confession in the Garden

In another very powerful scene from the third film, Michael Corleone is speaking to an old priest outside a beautiful church building bordered with flowers. The priest picks a stone from a fountain, and asks Corleone to look at it. He smashes it open, and shows him that even though it's been in water, the stone is bone dry inside. This, he says, is exactly the same as the people of Europe. They have been surrounded by the Christian faith, and yet Jesus does not live within them.

The priest offers to hear the Michael's confession.

'But it's been too long', argues Corleone. How can he repent after thirty years? He's convinced that he's beyond redemption.

The priest urges him to seize the moment: after all, what has Corleone got to lose? So he starts confessing.

He has betrayed his wife, he confesses.

The priest encourages him to continue. A bell tolls.

He has betrayed himself, too – by killing a man.

'Go on', says the priest once more.

Corleone hesitates. There is more: he ordered the killing of his own brother. He then begins to cry.

'Your sins are terrible', acknowledges the priest.

He speaks words of absolution in Latin, and once again, a bell tolls. This time, it's louder. Corleone is broken.

We Can All Change

For the past few years, *ER* has ranked among the most popular television series. In one episode, a white man was brought into the emergency room. The camera revealed a tattoo on his shoulder that read '*KKK*' – standing for Ku Klux Klan. It so happened that a black nurse was standing over the patient. The man looked up into the face of the woman and asked to be seen by a white nurse. His reason for doing so, however, was different from what we might first assume.

The white man explained to the black nurse, 'I didn't want you to look at the symbols that represent the animosity and hatred of my past. I'm saved now. I am a follower of Jesus Christ.'

The nurse was silent.

The man asked her, 'Do you think a person can truly change?'

She quietly replied, 'Yes, I do.'

It is worth asking three simple questions.

First, do you think a person can truly change? Is it really possible?

Second, do you need to change? Is there a habit that has you in its grip and from which you need to break free? Is there an attitude that you have been carrying that you need to let go of? Is there an activity that you have been involved in, that you need to quit?

Third, if you think people can change, and if you think you need to change, then how are you *going* to change? What will it take? Can you change by the sheer determination of your will? Can you change by keeping a positive mental attitude? Do you simply need a good example to follow?

What will it take for you to really change?

People *can* change, and there isn't a single person who doesn't need to change in some way. But it will take more than the force of our own will, more than a positive attitude and more than a good example to follow. For us to truly change, we need to recognise the extraordinary act of love that God has demonstrated in the death of his Son. We must see the great lengths that God the Father has gone to in order that we might be reconciled to him and be a part of his family forever.

Mary Ann Bird told of a childhood experience that changed her life forever.

> 'I grew up knowing I was different and I hated it,' she said. 'I was born with a cleft palate, and when I started school, my classmates made it clear to me how I looked. When I was asked, 'What happened to your lip?' I'd tell them that I had fallen and cut it on a piece of glass. Somehow, it seemed more acceptable to have suffered an accident, than to have been born different.
>
> 'I was convinced that no one outside my family could love me. There was however, a teacher in the second grade that we all adored – Mrs Leonard. Annually, we had a hearing test. Mrs Leonard gave the test to everyone in the class, and finally it was my turn. I knew, from past years, that as we stood against the door and covered one ear, the teacher sitting at her desk would whisper something and we would repeat it back. She'd whisper things like, "The sky is blue" or "Do you have new shoes?"
>
> 'I waited for those words, those seven words that changed my life.
>
> Mrs Leonard said, in her whisper,
>
> "I wish you were my little girl."'

Cords of Heavenly Love

Every one of us has been deformed, ever since our strings were severed from God. But God desires each one of us to be his daughter or his son. His love is sufficient to begin to change our lives. God loves us with a love that will not let us go, even though everyone else may choose to give up on us. This is good news!

However, we also need to ask ourselves how we avoid just turning into fake Christians. After all, that's not real change. As we said, it's not enough to go through the motions, or to mouth religious platitudes.

So, first, we need to be inwardly changed by Christ, not just externally conformed to his teaching or to the culture of the church. Then, we need to allow the presence of God, through his Holy Spirit, to work in us and produce good 'fruit'. We need to be honest with ourselves, honest with each other, and we need to be honest with God. The whole process begins by 'repenting', which means turning away from everything we know is wrong and turning to Jesus.

Nobel's Legacy

The Nobel Peace Prize is the supreme award given to those who have made an exceptional contribution to improving the world. Other Nobel Prizes are given to those who have made outstanding contributions in the arts and sciences.

Alfred Nobel was a Swedish chemist, who made his fortune by inventing powerful explosives and licensing the formula to governments to make weapons.

One day, Nobel's brother died, and a newspaper, in error, printed an obituary notice for Alfred, instead of his deceased brother. It 'remembered' Alfred as the inventor of dynamite: a man who made his fortune by enabling armies to achieve new levels of mass destruction.

Alfred had a unique opportunity to read his own obituary and to see how he would be remembered. He was shocked to think that he would ultimately be recorded in history as a merchant of death and destruction. So, he used his fortune to establish the awards, for accomplishments, which we know today and which contribute to the furtherance of life, not death. Nobel is remembered for his contribution to peace and human achievement – not, as he originally feared, as the man who pedalled death and destruction to the masses.

Nobel had spent much of his life being 'successful' in the business world, only to realise that he had made a huge mistake. Like Scrooge in Charles Dickens' *A Christmas Carol*, he got a glimpse of the future, and he didn't like what he saw.

If people who know you could write your obituary, what would they write? If you were incredibly honest, how would you write your own? Why don't you try? It could change the way you see your life – for good.

Will you let Christ hold the strings of your life? Will you let Christ heal your broken threads? Although most of us are nowhere near as bad as Don Corleone and his family, we all engage in little acts of wrongdoing that are the first link in a chain of destruction. All of us feel the need to repent, and many of us struggle with the idea that anyone could forgive us.

The good news is that God, through his son Jesus, is able to forgive everything we have done, no matter how bad. And in doing so, he welcomes us into the ultimate family – the family of God.

2

In Search of Father

LARA CROFT, TOMB RAIDER

Mark Stibbe

2001, Paramount

Director:
Simon West

Starring:
Angelina Jolie
John Voight
Ian Glen
Noah Taylor
Daniel Craig

Classification: 12

Sometimes you find yourself sitting in a cinema watching a movie that isn't particularly good. You wonder why you have chosen to see it at all! But then, just when you least expect it, something touches you deeply. A piece of dialogue, a moving act of sacrifice, a great piece of camera work, and before you know it, you have been impacted spiritually.

The film we are going to look at now provides an example of how this can happen. It is *Lara Croft, Tomb Raider*, directed by Simon West, and starring Angelina Jolie and John Voight.

This is not a great film. One critic said 'Right now, my greatest fear in life is hearing the words, "*Tomb Raider 2*"'. Another film critic commented that 'it feels as if it was edited by Edward Scissorhands'. Another critic, perhaps most damming of all, said, 'This is this year's *Battlefield Earth*' (a film with John Travolta that bombed at the box office).

Yet, at the same time, this film moved me spiritually, and it did so because of the relationship between the two main stars, Angelina Jolie and John Voight. These two actors play daughter and father in the plot, but they are also daughter and father in real life. Throughout the movie, Lara Croft (Angelina Jolie) mourns the death of her father, Lord Richard Croft (John Voight). Yet, through an ancient artefact that controls time, she manages to restore contact for a brief moment with her dad, in order to express the real feelings of her heart. *Tomb Raider* is therefore more than just an action and adventure film. It is also a story of how a daughter searched for the father in her life. This search not only took place in the story of the film. It also took place in production, as daughter and father worked together.

A Female Indiana Jones

The story of the film is based on the violent Tomb Raider computer games. These games, designed for the Sony Playstation, are a cultural phenomenon in their own right. In the games, Lara Croft functions as a female version of Indiana Jones, looking for ancient artefacts in exotic locations, battling against all kinds of enemies.

Director Simon West transferred her from computer to cinema, and in doing so, the film earned more in its first weekend than any other movie with a female lead. You probably ought not to be overly impressed by this statistic. The film that held this honour before Tomb Raider was *Charlie's Angels!*

Nevertheless, its success does indicate the degree to which Lara Croft has become something of a role model for Generation X.

So what's the story? Lara Croft is entrusted with the task of finding and destroying an artefact that gives its user the power to control time. Her enemies are called the Illuminati, which is Latin for enlightened ones. They are a secret society of rich men who will stop at nothing to get hold of this missing treasure in order to use it for their own evil ends.

Lara Croft embarks on her mission because of a letter from her father Lord Richard Croft, which arrives years after his death. Her father's solicitors have been instructed to post it to her on a certain date and the letter arrives at the Croft country estate.

Clip One:A Letter from Father

A postman brings a letter to Lara who sits down in shock. 'It's from my father', she cries. 'It was written before he died and delivered today as per his instructions'.

The letter contains some lines from a William Blake poem, written in Lord Croft's own hand:

> To see a world in a grain of sand
> And a heaven in a wild flower
> To hold infinity in the palm of your hand
> And eternity in an hour

This leads Lara to her father's library where she finds an old leather-bound edition of *The Writings of William*

Blake. She pulls it from the shelf and starts to look through its pages. Hidden in the back cover is another letter, also from her father.

'My Darling Daughter

I knew you would figure this out. If you're reading this letter, I am no longer with you and I miss you and love you always and forever. It also means I have failed and must place an awful burden on your shoulders.'

The letter continues with Lord Croft asking his daughter to discover and reconnect the two parts of a magical triangle of light. If these two pieces fall into the wrong hands, it spells disaster for the planet. But if Lara can get there first and dispose forever of this artefact, then the world will be saved from the wicked Illuminati. The letter finishes with these words:

'So Lara, I'm asking you to complete my work. Find and destroy both halves of the triangle.'

The next moment we see Lara preparing to leave for Cambodia to seek out the first half of the triangle. She is dressed in a white T-shirt with a red cross painted on it.

Searching for Father

While the main plot of the movie revolves around the search for the two pieces of the triangle (with Lara inevitably triumphing), the sub-plot concerns Lara's search for her father. Already, before the scene described above, Lara has gone to a small plaque on the ground outside her house. The plaque simply reads:

LORD RICHARD CROFT
Missing in the Field
May 15 1985 – Lost but Never Forgotten

Lara had said there, 'I miss you Daddy. I wish we could get back the time that was stolen from us'.

Now, having discovered the letter from her father, Lara's relationship with her absent father becomes a significant theme in the narrative of the film. Not only is she seeking to retrieve the triangle to prevent the Illuminati from controlling time, she now also hopes that her discovery of the artefact will enable her to reclaim the time with her father that has been so tragically stolen from her.

In the light of all this, some viewers may sense similarities between Lara Croft and Jesus. Jesus also came to embark on a quest given to him by his Heavenly Father. In John 5:36, Jesus said that his job was to do the will of his Father who sent him and to finish his work. From a place beyond time, Lara's father says, 'I'm asking you to complete my work'. The cross on Lara's T-shirt reminds the viewer that Jesus' work entailed him dying at Calvary.

A Case of Art Imitating Life

The star of *Lara Croft, Tomb Raider* is Angelina Jolie. Her full name is Angelina Jolie Voight. She was born in 1975. Her parents separated when she was a toddler and she was raised by her mother, Marcheline Bertrand. She studied film, she became a model and she starred in a number of pop videos before embarking on a career as a film actress. She married and then divorced. She recently married a film star called Billy Bob Thornton (his fifth marriage). They met on the set of a film they both starred in called *Pushing Tin*.

Angelina Jolie has been voted one of the fifty most beautiful women in the world by *People Magazine*. Yet, underneath her undeniably attractive and successful appearance, there is a troubled heart. She once said to a reporter, 'I see people with kids or married or in love and think that's great. But it's not my life and I wish I could have that, but I'm never going to have that because I'm all over the place. I'm never going to be calm or stable or normal or safe'.

At the heart of her unhappiness was her parent's divorce. This led to a difficult relationship with her actor father John Voight (aged 62 at the time of the movie). Like many people who suffer from 'absent father syndrome', this caused Jolie to strive even harder for success, perhaps at least in part to earn her father's attention and admiration. This duly came when in 1999 she won an Oscar for her role in the film *Girl Interrupted*. In Jolie's acceptance speech she said these words 'and my dad', referring to John Voight. 'You're a great actor but you're a better father'. This comment highlights the degree to which the two have made efforts to re-establish the relationship that was tragically disrupted in Jolie's childhood.

Simon West, the director of Lara Croft, decided to put these two actors together for his movie. On the 'Special Features' section of the Lara Croft DVD, there is a very revealing segment entitled, 'Digging Into Tomb Raider'. There is an interview with Simon West. Lloyd Levin, the producer, introduces the director's remarks by saying, 'At the centre of this global adventure, the core of the story is about a daughter's relationship with her father'. Simon West then gives the following insights: 'I had to look for someone that would measure up to Angelina. I thought, "Well, why not her *real* father, John Voight?" Again, I wasn't sure whether they actually would want to work together, so I kind of approached them separately and they loved the idea. And that just worked so well because they're having these emotional scenes between a father and a daughter and they *really are* a father and a daughter, so they're completely real'.

At this point, Jolie herself comments: 'It's a very special thing, because our relationship is very, very similar to these two people. They have similar loves, they have a similar sense of adventure, and they want to set things right. They're curious about life, curious about the past'.

It's interesting to me that in another press interview Angelina Jolie said that she performed the breathtaking stunts in the film in order to impress her father and that the film was a means of reconciliation for them. In fact, the two of them often had to stop in the scenes that they were filming together because they would keep crying. Jolie said it was an extraordinarily intensive emotional experience for her. It was a case of art imitating life.

Our Father in Heaven

This idea of 'searching for the father' provides a great way into the spiritual significance of the movie. Obviously, the film is in itself very spiritual in content. There is a very strong vein of mysticism throughout. In fact, Christian viewers will have to trawl through quite a lot of eastern mystical imagery before locating the specifically Christian parallels. In this respect, the film is a typical example of our post-modern 'pick-'n'-mix' culture, with its little bit of New Age, Hinduism, Buddhism, Christianity, and so on. The film does not attempt to privilege one religious tradition over another. They all simply co-exist in a world where all religions appear to be one.

Nevertheless, from a Christian point of view, perhaps the most important theme has to do with 'searching for the father'. Jesus came to reveal God as Father. He revealed that God is relational, not remote, longing for his estranged children to be reconciled to him. He showed us that God is a Father who is forever faithful.

Jesus told a parable about a young man, who asked his dad for his inheritance, left home, lived a life of excessive indulgence in a foreign land, lost everything and then came to his senses. Far away from home, he longed to be reunited with his father. So, he began a long journey home, not knowing whether his father would accept or reject him. In Luke 15, the chapter where the story is told, we see that in fact the father has been waiting for years for his son to come home. We read in verse 20 of Luke 15: 'While he was still a long distance away, his father saw him coming. Filled with love and compassion he ran to his son, embraced him, and kissed him'.

Jesus told this parable to show us both what we are like and what God is like. We are like rebellious children who have rejected God and wandered far away from him. But God is like a father, a perfect patient extravagantly loving dad, who runs to embrace us when we repent, when we say sorry and turn back to him. Jesus came to restore relationship with our Father in heaven. He said 'I am the way, the truth, and the life. No one can come to the Father except through me' (John 14:6).

Clip Two: Daughter and Father Together Again

In the one moment of genuine emotion in the Lara Croft movie, Lara meets up with her dead father in a place beyond time. The two pieces of the triangle of light are now reunited and Lara finds herself able to control time. She speaks with her father:

LARA: Daddy
CROFT: Lara
LARA: Is this real?
CROFT: It is a crossing. My past and your present.
LARA: Why did you not tell me about the Illuminati?
CROFT: You were only a child.
LARA: You could have written in your journals. You never mentioned it. Not once.
CROFT: Lara, I burst to tell you everything. But in the fierceness of my own battles I strove to tell you only that which would inspire you and keep you safe. I love you so much.
LARA: I've missed you.
CROFT: And I have missed you. I know why you came here. Why you took the power of the light. But this must not happen.
LARA: Why? Why can't we use the power just this once?

Why can't you stay?
CROFT: We can't change time.
LARA: But time was stolen from us. And it's not fair.
CROFT: No it's not fair. But you have stolen time itself and you must give it back. You must destroy the triangle.
LARA: Suddenly I feel so alone.
CROFT: You're never alone. I am with you always just as I've always been.

The scene ends with the father reaching out his right hand to his daughter, she reaching out her left hand to him, the two hands touching (like Michelangelo's *Creation of Adam*), and light bursting from the contact.

There's something very Christian about that scene, especially the Father's words, 'I am with you always'. Is this not what Jesus came to reveal about God? That he is a father who will never abandon us if we choose to follow his Son? In Hebrews 13:5 we read, 'God has said, "Never will I leave you; never will I forsake you"'. God will never be an absent father for those who truly seek him.

Healing the 'Father' Wounds Within

So many people today have very deep parental wounds in their lives. Just after Christmas on 29 December 2001, I bought a copy of the Saturday edition of the *Daily Telegraph* and opened up to the colour supplement. On the front was a photograph of a young girl and the headline 'Children Left Behind'. It was all about the children who have been bereaved as a result of the terrorist attacks on America on 11 September 2001.

Over five thousand children lost a parent in the twin towers tragedy. The article was a heartbreaking and harrowing account of some of these children's tragedies, particularly those that had lost fathers.

One of the men killed in the twin towers, Christopher Wodenshek, had five children. His eight-year-old daughter Hayley was particularly devastated. 'She cries a lot', said her mother, 'and she doesn't want to go to school. In fact, she doesn't want to believe it's true. She said, "Well Mummy, in *Cast Away* the man came back after four years". And I said, "Honey, that was a movie"'.

Life of course is not a movie.

What hope is there for those who have a father-shaped hole in their hearts? I really believe that the hope is in Jesus, who reveals God as Father. When you become a Christian you are reconciled to a Father who will never leave you nor forsake you, who will always be there for you and whose love is not earned through impressive stunts, but just simply given. The fact is, we have a perfect Father beyond time in heaven, who has made his love known to us through Jesus, and who has made himself ever-present to our hearts in the person of his Holy Spirit.

Jesus came to finish a work that his Father had given him. That work was to die upon a cross. All you and I have to do is to decide to come back home to God. In Luke 15:18 the son who ran away from home said this 'I will go home to my Father and say, "Father I have sinned against both heaven and you"'.

All you need to do is seek the Father, and you will find him.

Everlasting Arms of Love

Last year I spoke at a conference in Canada. My subject was the Fatherhood of God. After I had spoken about the intimate love of God, I asked people to respond and receive prayer if they felt that they had never known God as Father.

One man, in his late sixties, was sitting with his back to the stage and he was weeping. He told me that his dad had died when he was four years old. He had never – in sixty years – felt the embrace of a father. Not until that evening. During the message, he had started praying as he sat listening. Suddenly he felt strong and loving arms around him. He looked, but no one was there. He closed his eyes. Once again, those arms of love held and enfolded him. He realised that it was his Heavenly Father and he cried for joy. His parting words to me were, 'I'm so glad that God is relational, not remote.'

If you are prepared to search for the Father, if you are prepared to come running home in true repentance, you will find God's arms are open wide for you. God is a perfect Father who is always there for you. Through Jesus, he has revealed his love to the world. By his Holy Spirit, he makes this love a reality in our hearts, so that we too can hear the words: 'You're never alone. I am with you always just as I've always been'.

3

The Dance of Life

BILLY ELLIOT

J. John

2000, Universal

Director:
Stephen Daldry

Starring:
Jamie Bell
Julie Walters
Gary Lewis

Classification: 15

Can you remember how good it felt as a child to jump up and down on your bed? It seemed, back then, to be the most wonderful experience in the world. In true abandonment, you were free to be yourself, to let both your body and spirit soar. That is, at least until your parents heard you doing so and ordered you to stop.

I remember my bed-jumping days, and I wonder why and where they've gone. As adults, we seem to lose the ability to 'wonder', to marvel at the goodness of life that the Creator has given us. We've forgotten how to jump, and we have silenced the voice of awe and amazement – the voice of God – which has always been speaking to us, even before we were born.

Billy Elliot and the Dance of Life

As the film *Billy Elliot* opens, we see our hero (played by Jamie Bell) jumping, or rather, leaping around on his bed, without a care in the world. He seems to have been created for movement.

Billy Elliot is a film that evokes both laughter and tears. It offers a stark picture of reality, while delivering the message that hope can triumph over despair, and beauty over ugliness. This is why it took everyone by surprise and became such a 'big' movie, which ended up winning 'best film' at the 2000 British Academy Awards (Jamie Bell won 'best actor' too), and being nominated for Oscars.

This is a film about being who you were created to be and about being transformed. Billy is an 11-year-old boy living in a coal-mining town in the North-East of England in 1984, at the time of the crippling miner's strike. His family are struggling painfully to make ends meet, as the two breadwinners, his father and brother, are both out on the picket line.

Billy is a skinny boy, and to toughen him up, his dad makes him take boxing lessons. He's never going to be the next Rocky, though, and one day at the gym, he notices a ballet class which is being taught by a tough-minded teacher, Mrs Wilkinson (Julie Walters). Her young daughter dares Billy to join in, and gradually he becomes enthralled and passionate about dancing. However, he keeps his lessons a secret from his battle-hardened family, who are increasingly desperate to put food on the table as the strike drags on.

When his father finally learns the truth about the dancing, he forbids him from continuing with the class, sparking a family crisis in the process. Billy tries to demonstrate that dance is more than just a hobby for him – it's a dream. Against the odds, and amid an intimidating, macho atmosphere, Billy holds on to that dream, and keeps dancing.

So what drives him? It is the love of his mother, who, before she died the previous year, gave Billy a letter that she instructed him not to open until he reached 18. Unable to wait, the 11-year-old opened and memorised it.

Clip One: Opening the Letter

In one of the most powerful scenes in the film, Mrs Wilkinson is alone in the gym, when Billy joins her. She swings a punch bag, and they go to sit down on the dusty boxing ring floor. Billy has some personal things to show her: a football shirt, a tape, and an envelope. Mrs Wilkinson looks at it, with curiosity.

'It's a letter,' says Billy. She knows it's a letter, but what's it about? Billy explains that his mum wrote it for him before she died. He gives it to Mrs Wilkinson, who opens it and begins to read, 'To my son, Billy …'

As she reads, Billy, who knows his mother's words off by heart, joins in. Mrs Wilkinson puffs on her cigarette, and looks at Billy, her motherly instinct reaching out in this moment of profound sadness. Billy looks lost and wistful, and rests his head, in resignation, on the ropes.

Billy's mum wrote, 'Please know that I was always with you through everything. I always will be. I'm proud to have known you, and I'm proud you were mine. Always be yourself. I'll love you forever. Mum.'

Making the Most of Time

We can probably sympathise with the words on a tombstone that read, 'I expected this, but not yet.' The Bible, however, warns us against complacency. In James' epistle, he asks his readers, 'How do you know what will happen tomorrow? For your life is like the morning fog – it's here a little while, then it's gone' (James 4:14). We know that death can come at any time: by design, disease, or disaster . . . It's just that we think it probably won't happen to us. Not yet, anyway. *Billy Elliot* reminds us that death can strike any time.

A minister once stood to speak at the funeral of his friend. He referred to the dates that had been carved on her tombstone: the beginning and the end of her life. He noted that the first date signified her birth . . . but then spoke of the next date, her end, with tears. However, he said that what mattered most of all was the 'dash' that was scored between those two years. The dash represented all the time that she spent alive on earth, and only those who loved her could understand what that little line was worth.

> It doesn't really matter how much we own – the cars, the house, the cash.
> What matters is how we live and love and how we spend our 'dash'.
> If only we could slow down just enough to consider what's true and real,
> And always try to understand the way other people feel.
> If only we could treat each other with respect, and more often wear a smile,

Remembering that this special 'dash' might only last a little while.

So, when your eulogy is being read, with your life's actions to rehash . . .

Would you be pleased with the things they say, about how you spent your 'dash'?

Responding to Our Troubles

Throughout the film, we catch glimpses of difficulty, disappointment, discouragement and despair. No doubt, we have all experienced those words and their effects in some way. An army chaplain once had a sign on his door that read, 'If you have troubles, come in and tell me about them. If you don't have troubles, come in and tell me how you do it.'

Billy's family is familiar with troubles. In the film, winter arrives. The family now finds itself out of coal, and in order to keep everyone warm, Billy's father is forced to chop up his wife's treasured piano for firewood.

Clip Two: Chopping up Mum's Piano

Picture the scene: it's Christmas. Outside, the snow is falling heavily; it's a romantic, winter, wonderland. But when you have no fuel to heat your house, Christmas snow is a curse, not a blessing. In the social club, the miners gather in a show of solidarity to wish each other happy Christmas. But Billy's dad is not among them. He is in his backyard, with a sledgehammer, swinging methodically and painfully at his wife's old piano. They must, and shall have warmth on Christmas Day. Billy lurks in the background. He asks his dad if he thinks she'll mind. 'Shut it, Billy. She's dead,' he replies coldly. And with that, he swings again, crying out as he does so.

We cut to Christmas dinner. Not your traditional dinner, as the family aren't sitting around a table, but balancing their paltry dishes on their laps. The focus of the scene is the blazing fire, giving warmth and light. It is as though Billy's mum is there in the room, her presence lighting their silent gathering. Yet, the flames just serve to illuminate her absence. Billy's father breaks the silence. 'Merry Christmas,' he says. 'Merry Christmas,' they reply.

And then, in the silence, Billy's dad finally betrays his true emotions. He begins to sob, as the fire crackles . . . Sitting next to the fire, the father finally shows that his heart is broken. His sorrows overwhelm him.

The scene reminds me of Psalm 51, which says, 'The sacrifice you want is a broken spirit. A broken and repentant heart, O God, you will not despise' (Psalm 51:17).

Clip Three: Dancing for Dad

Billy's father and his mate are walking through the snow back home, past the gym. His mate looks in through the window, and sees Billy dancing with his best friend, who is dressed comically in a tutu. They are having fun, lost in dancing. Billy's dad walks into the gym, out of the cold. The embarrassment is tangible for everyone, and Billy's friend wriggles out of his tutu. Billy stares at his dad, yet neither of them talk: they are both utterly lost for words. So Billy decides to let his feet do the talking. He starts to dance. Aggressively, at first, in his dad's face. It's as though he's saying, 'This is me – I am your son.' Take me or leave me, but this is who I am. And then he fills the room with movement, dancing beautifully, gracefully, yet clearly with strength and muscle, too. Billy is strong; he is becoming a man. His dance ends back in front of his father. He stops, with a flourish, triumphantly. Silence. His friend claps, tentatively. Billy's dad turns and leaves – again, without a word. He trudges off through the snow, unable to process or understand quite what he's just seen. That was his son in there: should he be proud, or humiliated? Billy runs out, after him. He shouts at the top of his voice down the street, standing in the ice and snow in just shorts and a T-shirt. 'Dad!' The silence is broken …

Billy's father is finally won over, and sets about making huge sacrifices to ensure Billy can go to the Royal Ballet School. He apologises to the ballet teacher, Mrs Wilkinson. He humbles himself and breaks the picket line, which brings about a cathartic moment with his eldest son. And he sells his wife's jewellery in order to get Billy to London.

Billy receives confirmation of his place at the Royal Ballet School the same day as the strike is called off. And the new life for Billy brings new life to the entire family.

The film ends with a truly great scene.

Clip Four: Dancing on Stage

The theatre is grand and imposing. This is the big city; this is where it's at. Billy's dad and brother, older now, take their seats. His father asks a member of staff to let Billy Elliot know that his family are here. We cut to backstage. Dancers wait, made-up and in costume, in the wings. The producer approaches the man who is clearly the star. He is strong and well built, his muscles beautifully defined.

'Billy, your family are here.'

He looks, thinks, smiles. Then he stretches one last time, as the other dancers take their cue and take the stage. This is his moment. All eyes are upon him. He enters the stage, and leaps towards the heavens. This is it. In front of the crowd. In the spotlight. Before his family at last. This is his moment. This is Billy Elliot.

The Transforming Power of God

'You have turned my mourning into joyful dancing. You have taken away my clothes of mourning and clothed me with joy, that I might sing praises to you and not be silent. O Lord my God, I will give you thanks forever' (Psalm 30:11–12).

How has God turned our mourning into dancing? God is the author of life, the creator of light, the pillar of truth. Friedrich Nietzsche once wrote, 'I would believe only in a God that knows how to dance.' Well, the good news is, he does. God expressed his life, light and truth in Jesus, and as we connect with him, we connect with life, light and truth. His life inspires us to tap into our God-given creativity and experience life abundantly. To experience his light and dispel any darkness that hinders us. To experience the truth, to release us from the lies about who we are, and what we can (or can't) achieve.

The actor Peter Sellers once appeared on *The Muppet Show* and was interviewed by Kermit the Frog. Kermit told him, 'Peter, now just relax and be yourself.'

Sellers responded, 'I can't be myself because I don't know who I am. The real me doesn't exist.'

Six months after that interview, he died.

It's probably true that many of us go through life wondering who we are, what we're supposed to be doing and where we're going. Since our days are numbered, it is wise to seek perspective from the God of eternity. My experience of Jesus Christ is that he is life, light and truth. The dark moment that the caterpillar calls the end of the world, is the sun-filled moment that the butterfly calls the beginning. The most delightful surprise in my life was suddenly to recognise my worth in God's eyes. I became really alive.

Fulfilling Your God-given Destiny

A dead fish can float downstream, but it takes a live one to swim upstream.

The *Billy Elliot* story shows the rewards of perseverance in following our dreams and not giving up, especially in the face of hostile popular opinion. The word persevere is comprised of the prefix 'per', meaning 'through', and the word 'severe'. It means to keep pressing on, even through difficult circumstances. Trying times are not the times to stop trying. Don't pray for an easier life; pray to be a stronger person.

Life is like a ten-speed bike. Most of us have gears we never use. We can't do much about the length of our life, but we can do a lot about its depth.

Two men went fishing. Every time one fisherman caught a big fish, he put it in his icebox to keep it fresh. Whenever the other fisherman caught a big fish, he threw it back.

His friend asked, 'Why do you keep throwing back all the big fish you catch?'

The fisherman replied, 'I only have a small frying pan.'

Sometimes, like that fisherman, we throw back the big plans, big dreams, big opportunities that God gives us. Our faith is too small.

How could that fisherman not figure out that all he needed was a bigger frying pan? Whether it is a possibility or a problem, God will never give us anything bigger than we can handle. That means we can walk confidently into anything God brings our way. We can do all things through Christ who strengthens us (Philippians 4:13).

Whatever your past has been, you have a spotless future.

The winds of God are always blowing, but we must set the sails.

4

THE VALUE OF A SINGLE LIFE

SAVING PRIVATE RYAN

Mark Stibbe

1998, Paramount and Dreamworks
Director:
Steven Spielberg
Starring:
Tom Hanks
Tom Sizemore
Edward Burns
Barry Pepper
Adam Goldberg
Classification: 15

Erich Fromm once said, 'People are born equal but they are also born different'. In other words, every person is a unique individual, infinitely precious in the sight of God. Thomas Fuller, in an age when the group was superseding the individual in terms of rights said it this way: 'a whole bushel of wheat is made up of individual grains'. Community is critical to the future of humanity, yes, but not at the expense of individuality. Few if any have put it better than Mother Teresa: 'To us what matters is an individual. . . . I believe in person to person. Every person is Christ for me, and since there is only one Jesus, that person is the only person in the world for me at that moment.'

Leaving Ninety Nine to Search for One

Jesus taught and demonstrated the value of a single life. For him, every individual was of inestimable value. Every individual, however ordinary and sinful, was worth saving. As he said, 'the Son of Man' [referring to himself] 'came to seek and to save the lost'.

To underline the point Jesus told a story about a sheep that wandered off from its flock (18:12–14): 'What do you think? If a man owns a hundred sheep, and one of them wanders away, will he not leave the ninety-nine on the hills and go to look for the one that wandered off? And if he finds it, I tell you the truth, he is happier about that one sheep than about the ninety-nine that did not wander off. In the same way your Father in heaven is not willing that any of these little ones should be lost'.

A parable is really an earthly story illustrating a heavenly truth. Here the heavenly truth being illustrated is the value of a single life. Jesus tells of a shepherd who leaves ninety-nine sheep in order to find one sheep that has got lost. He leaves ninety-nine on the hills on their own, vulnerable and without protection, in order to find just one. He does not leave the ninety-nine safe in a sheepfold or a barn. He leaves them on the hills where robbers, wolves and bears had every chance of finding them. How foolish can you get!

My friend J. John, co-author of this book, has a great way of making Bible truths very relevant and fresh. When he speaks on this passage, he explains it like this.

Imagine you have five hundred pounds in five-pound notes. You have them all together and you hold them close to your chest. You are so happy with these bank notes. You won't let them out of your sight. You take them to bed with you. You take them everywhere with you. You are extremely attached to them. One day you go out for a long walk in the hills. You sit down for a rest on a bench and in an idle moment, you start counting them. Unfortunately, the wind gets up and one of the five-pound notes blows away. You decide you can't bear to live without the one that's lost, so you leave all the other ninety-nine five-pound notes on the bench and you wander off to find the one lost. At last, you find it and return to the other ninety-nine notes, reuniting them. You laugh and dance and shout for joy. This is not because you found the ninety-nine still on the bench where you left them, but because you found the one that had blown away!

Put like this, you can see the humour and the surprise in the parable. You can see the reckless love of our Father in heaven, who rejoices over just one lost person being found and rescued.

The Value of the Individual

Spielberg is one of the most famous and successful film directors of all time. It has been said that the most beautiful words you can read on a film screen are, 'A film by Steven Spielberg'.

Spielberg has for a long time been interested in the value of a single life. Think of his movie about the Holocaust, *Schindler's List*. This film tells the true story of Oscar Schindler, a non-Jewish businessman who rescues many Jews from the Nazi concentration camps. At the end of the movie, some of his rescuers present Schindler with a gold ring. Inside the ring is inscribed in Hebrew, 'He who saves a single life saves the world entire'. Clearly, the value of a single life is a key theme in *Schindler's List*.

To prove the point, remember that the movie is filmed in black and white. Yet, from time to time, a young girl appears wearing a red coat. The coat itself is in colour while the rest of the picture is not. The reason for this recurring image is critical. This 'singling' out of a solitary child through the use of colour brings into the foreground Spielberg's preoccupation with the value of a single life. It is the camera's way of saying, 'Look, she's important'.

Saving Private Ryan is another World War II movie that explores the same theme. This film earned Spielberg an Oscar for Best Director, and was also awarded four other Academy Awards. It is commonly regarded as the most graphic war film ever made.

The film tells the story of Captain John Miller, who is sent on a mission after the D Day landings in June 1944. Having successfully landed on Omaha beach, Miller is sent with a small squad of soldiers to locate a Private James Ryan. Ryan's three other brothers have been killed in action and so it is decided that James Ryan must be rescued. It is simply inconceivable that a mother should lose all four sons. So Miller takes his squad on a journey of suffering, all in search of just one solitary life. Not a general, not a spy, or a politician – just a private!

Here again, we see Spielberg's fascination with the idea of the value of the individual. In the great chaos of war, where human beings fight each other *en masse*, where names are often forgotten, where individuality becomes increasingly irrelevant, Spielberg chooses to remind us that every person counts. Every gravestone, every cross, every memorial has individual names representing unique life histories with unrepeatable memories. Every 'dog tag' is a symbol of a life, a soul, a person that will never again visit the stage of human history. This means that individuals count. They are worth rescuing. Or, to use the favoured metaphor of the film title, they are worth 'saving'. As the words on the theatrical trailer read, 'In the last great invasion of the last Great War, the greatest danger facing eight men was saving . . . *one*'.

Clip One: The Decision to Save One Man

After a harrowing re-enactment of the Omaha landings, the scene switches to the War Department back in the United States. The authorities discover that three Ryan brothers have been killed and so they speak to their commanding officer, General Marshall.

GENERAL MARSHALL: Ah, damn it.

COLONEL 1: All four of them were in the same company in the 29th division but we split them up after the Sullivan brothers died on the Juno.

GENERAL MARSHALL: Any contact with the fourth son, James?

COLONEL 1: No, sir. He was dropped about fifteen miles inland near Neuville. But that's still deep behind enemy lines.

COLONEL 2: There's no way you can know where in the hell he was dropped. General, first reports are that the 101st is scattered all to hell and gone. There are misdrops all over Normandy. Now assuming that Private Ryan even survived the jump, he could be anywhere. In fact, he's probably KIA [killed in action].

And frankly sir, we go sending some sort of rescue mission, flat heading throughout swarms of German reinforcements all along our axis of advance, they're going to be KIA too.

GENERAL MARSHALL: [Pauses, walks to his desk, picks out an old book, and extracts a letter from it.] I have a letter here, written a long time ago to a Mrs Bixby in Boston. So bear with me. [Reads]

'Dear Madam,

I have been shown in the files of the War Department by the Adjutant General of Massachusetts that you are the mother of five sons who have died gloriously on the field of battle.

I feel how weak and fruitless must be any words of mine that would attempt to beguile you from the grief of a loss so overwhelming. But I cannot refrain from tendering to you the consolation that may be found in the thanks of the Republic they died to save.

I pray that our Heavenly Father may assuage the anguish of your bereavement and leave you only the cherished memories of the loved and lost, the solemn pride that must be yours to have made so costly a sacrifice upon the altar of freedom.

Yours very sincerely and respectfully

Abraham Lincoln'

[Pauses.]

If the boy's alive, we are going to send somebody to find him. And we are going to get him the hell out of there.

It is with this scene that the plan to rescue Ryan is put into action. Everything depends upon the audience being persuaded, not only by the moving pictures of mother Ryan's obvious shock (played out just before this scene), but also General Marshall's trump card of the Lincoln letter. In a sense, the comments made by the second Colonel are apposite. It is a foolhardy and irrational idea to rescue Private James Ryan. The rescuers would stand little chance, and in any case, Ryan might well be dead already. The mission is set up here as fraught with problems. Yet, the ageing General Marshall takes a fatherly and compassionate perspective. Ryan is in a hell of a predicament (notice how the word 'hell' permeates the dialogue above) and he *must* be saved. Marshall does not want Mrs Ryan to lose *all* her sons. So he reads the letter written by Abraham Lincoln and the camera then zooms round the three other US officers, showing their obvious tacit agreement to the mission. Then he concludes with something of a rousing call to arms, 'We're going to get him the *hell* [this word is given emphasis] out of there'.

The Headquarters of Heaven

The Bible tells a story of salvation too. The name Jesus (Yeshua in the original language) literally means 'salvation'. God sent Jesus into the world to save us from our sins and to rescue us from the *hell* of a godless eternity. As the Gospel of John puts it, 'God so loved the world that he gave his only Son, so that everyone who believes in him will not perish but have eternal life' (John 3:16). The initiative for sending Jesus into the world to be our Saviour was God's. Our Heavenly Father made the decision. In the headquarters of heaven, God the Father came up with the rescue plan that brought us life.

A vicar was about to start his sermon during an evening service when he briefly introduced a visiting minister in the congregation. He said that the visitor was one of his dearest childhood friends and, accordingly, asked him to say a few words. With that, the elderly man walked to the pulpit and told a story:

'A father, his son, and a friend of his son were sailing off the Pacific coast when a fierce storm hit them and the three were swept into the sea as the boat capsized. Grabbing a rescue line, the father had to make the most painful decision of his life. Who was he to throw the lifeline to? The father knew his own son was a Christian and that the son's friend was not. The father yelled, 'I love you' to his boy and threw the line to the boy's friend, pulling him to safety, while his son disappeared forever beneath the waves. The father knew his son would step into eternity with Jesus, but couldn't bear the thought of the friend stepping into an eternity without Jesus. Therefore, he sacrificed his son to save the son's friend'.

Concluding, the visitor said, 'How great is God's love for us that he gave his only Son that we should be rescued. So take hold of the lifeline that the Father is throwing you in this service tonight'.

With that, the old man finished and the vicar took his place in the pulpit, and preached his message.

At the end of the meeting, some teenagers came up to the visitor. They had been looking very sceptical throughout the old man's story and had not responded to the appeal. 'That wasn't a very realistic story', they said mockingly. 'No dad would do that'.

'You've got a point', said the visitor. 'But I'm standing here tonight to tell you that this story gives me personally a great glimpse into the Father's love for us. You see. I was that father, and your Vicar here was my son's friend'.

The film *Saving Private Ryan* offers us a striking parable of the biblical drama of salvation. The avuncular and compassionate figure of General Marshall is like God the Father – beyond the battlefield, and yet deeply moved by the suffering of the people in his care. His role reminds us that God devised a rescue plan for us too. Our Heavenly Father could not live with the agony of seeing us torn apart by sin and death. So he asked his one and only Son to come as our Saviour. Not crossing an ocean and landing on a beach in France, but crossing from heaven to earth and touching down in Bethlehem. This was the Father's plan – to send his Son to invade enemy occupied territory. To fight against the evil one with the gospel of love and to rescue us from sin. This is what God is really like. He is a Father whose heart bleeds with compassionate love for his children. He is the perfect Father who loves with deeds not just with words.

The Saviour of Private Ryan

In *Saving Private Ryan,* it is General Marshall who has the plan, but it is Captain Miller, acted by Tom Hanks, who fulfils the mission. He chooses a team of eight men to find Private James Ryan. Hanks' portrayal of Captain Miller is nothing short of a masterpiece of acting. He manages to convey with commanding realism the way in which war throws ordinary people into extraordinary contexts, evoking extraordinary character traits. Hanks – now considered Hollywood's leading male actor – communicates in the most poignant way the role of the reluctant hero. It is hard to imagine anyone not being drawn into empathising with this married schoolteacher who becomes a brilliant, yet broken, leader of men.

When one of his rescue squad, Carpazo, has been killed by a sniper Miller starts to reminisce with his sergeant about Carpazo and about another soldier called Veccio, lost in a previous mission. The scene takes place in a church where the squad is billeted for the night. Captain Miller is 'confessing' to his sergeant the agony he feels over losing just one man. In the process of his confession, Miller offers his own rationale for the death of his soldiers and considers whether Private Ryan is worth the mission.

Clip Two: Confession in Church

CAPTAIN MILLER: Veccio, yeah. Carpazo. You see, when you end up killing one of your men, you tell yourself it happened so you could save the lives of two or three or ten others. Maybe a hundred others. But you know how many men I've lost under my command?

SERGEANT HORVATH: How many?

CAPTAIN MILLER: Ninety-four. But that means I've saved the lives of ten times that many. Doesn't it? Maybe even twenty. Right? Twenty times as many? And that's how simple it is. That's how you . . . how you rationalise making the choice between the mission and the man.

SERGEANT HORVATH: Except that this time the mission is a man.

CAPTAIN MILLER: This Ryan'd better be worth it. He'd better go home, cure some disease, or invent the longer lasting light bulb, or something. The truth is I wouldn't trade ten Ryans for one Veccio or one Carpazo.

SERGEANT HORVATH: Amen.

In this scene, Miller gives voice to Spielberg's overriding theme, the value of a single life. For Miller, it is important to remember the names and the idiosyncrasies of each of his men. The death of an individual soldier is a heartfelt event for Miller. It calls for an explanation. So, Miller reasons that one man dies to save others from dying – even up to as many as twenty others. The problem with the mission Miller is engaged in is that Ryan is not regarded in the same light. Ryan is an unknown quantity. 'He'd better be worth it', Miller states. He had better go back home after the war and earn his salvation. The truth is, ten Ryans would not be as valuable as one Veccio or one Carpazo.

Jesus' parable of the lost sheep illustrates beyond doubt that he considers individuals as uniquely precious and infinitely worth saving. The shepherd left ninety-nine sheep to rescue just one. Even though we were sinners in rebellion against God, wandering like sheep, Jesus pursued us out of love. We may be ordinary people like Private James Ryan, but Jesus Christ still came to rescue us, and he came willingly (not reluctantly) unlike Miller. He came for us as individuals.

Clip Three: The Supreme Sacrfice

In the end, Miller makes the supreme sacrifice for Ryan, as do most of his squad. The final scenes of the film are fraught with emotion. Miller has located Ryan behind enemy lines but Ryan has chosen to stay with his own men to defend a bridge. Miller and the remains of his squad stay with Ryan and together they hold the bridge at great cost.

Miller sits dying on the bridge, shot by a German soldier whom he had, ironically, set free earlier in the film when others had wanted to execute him. Miller says something under his breath and Ryan leans over to hear.

'James, earn this. Earn it'. These are Miller's last words.

The camera eventually focuses on the young Ryan's face as he stands over the body of his saviour. The voice of General Marshall is heard again reading the words of Abraham Lincoln's letter, quoted at the start of the film (the end returning to the beginning, as it were). Then the face of the young Ryan turns into the face of the elderly Ryan, fifty years later, standing at a cross with Captain John Miller's name on it in a war cemetery. Ryan is wracked with grief and guilt. He kneels and speaks to his dead rescuer: 'My family is with me today. They wanted to come with me. To be honest with you, I wasn't sure how I would feel coming back here. Every day I think about what you said to me that day on the bridge. I've tried to live my life the best I could. I hope that was enough. I hope that at least in your eyes I've earned what all of you have done for me'.

Ryan stands and his wife joins him. Ryan turns to her and asks, 'Tell me I've led a good life. . . . Tell me I'm a good man'.

The film ends with Ryan saluting. The camera lingers on the white cross that gives the briefest hint of the value of Miller's unique life.

JOHN H. MILLER
CAPT. 2 RANGERS BN
PENNSYLVANIA JUNE 13 1944

The final shot is of an American flag fluttering in the wind.

Salvation is a Free Gift

When I first saw this film in the cinema, I remember feeling uneasy as the dying Miller told Ryan to 'earn this'. As a Christian I believe without equivocation that our salvation is something freely given by God, not something earned through good works on our part. This is what the Apostle Paul wrote in his Letter to the Ephesians: 'Once you were dead, doomed forever because of your many sins. You used to live just like the rest of the world, full of sin, obeying Satan, the mighty prince of the power of the air. He is the spirit at work in the hearts of those who refuse to obey God. All of us used to live that way, following the passions and desires of our evil nature. We were born with an evil nature, and we were under God's anger just like everyone else' (2:1–3).

This is the bad news. But the good news is that Jesus came into the world to save us. We could not save ourselves, so Jesus did it for us on the Cross. And so Paul goes on to say, 'God saved you by his special favour when you believed. And you can't take credit for this; it is a gift from God. Salvation is not a reward for the good things we have done, so none of us can boast about it' (2:8–9).

Here we see the great difference between *Saving Private Ryan* and the New Testament. In *Saving Private Ryan,* salvation has to be earned. Miller insists that Ryan must earn what he has done for him, thereby condemning Ryan to fifty years tormented by guilt. 'Have I been good enough?' Ryan asks. All this as the camera ironically focuses on the cross – symbol and reminder of God's grace and that God has freely given us the gift of salvation. We cannot earn this salvation by works. We can only receive it by faith.

Saving Private Ryan has many parallels with the Christian message. Both the movie and Christianity are about the death of sons. Both explore the theme of sacrifice. Yet in the final analysis, Spielberg's theology is one in which salvation has to be earned. In the New Testament, the opposite is true. When the crucified Jesus cries 'It is finished', he is declaring that everything necessary for our salvation has been achieved. Nothing else is required. The price has been paid. All I need to do is say, 'I admit my need of salvation, I believe that Jesus has done everything necessary for me to be rescued, I choose to receive the free gift of forgiveness won for me when Jesus died, I decide now to ask Jesus into my life to be my Saviour, Lord and very best friend. I choose to follow him for the rest of my days'.

5

The Ship of Dreams

TITANIC

J. John

1997, 20th Century Fox

Director: James Cameron

Starring: Leonardo DiCaprio Kate Winslet

Classification: 12

I wasn't very keen to see *Titanic* when it first came out. A few particularly bad experiences of sea sickness in small boats, miles from land, coupled with thoughts of how terrifying it would have been to sink into the icy waters of the North Atlantic that fateful night in 1912, meant that I was not looking forward to watching the inevitable unfolding of a tragedy in which nearly fifteen hundred people died.

However, I was both surprised and moved by a film that turned out to be the most expensive to date, costing $200 million to make. The ill-fated voyage of the opulent ocean liner was represented on screen in all its glorious excess, thanks to the writing, directing and editing of James Cameron, together with a haunting soundtrack from James Horner. The film went on to receive fifteen Academy awards and was the top grossing film of all time, taking over $1.8 billion at the box office – double the amount of the previous record holder, *Jurassic Park*. It crossed the lines of age, gender and race in a way that few films seem to manage.

Titanic presents the fictional love story between Rose (Kate Winslet) and Jack Dawson (Leonardo DiCaprio) which takes place aboard the historical setting of the famously 'unsinkable' ship. It is a story that perhaps we can all, in some ways, relate to. Although, stereotypically, we think that young women are looking for romance from films, while men crave for adventure, in fact all of us, if we are honest, long for both.

This is a film of contrast and comparison. Cameron gives us both intimate details of the voyage and the grand spectacle of it all. He is able to contrast all that is arrogant and selfish in humanity with the sacrifice and dignity that we can, at our best, embody so nobly. Commenting on the film, he said, '*Titanic* is not just a cautionary tale – a myth, a parable, a metaphor for the ills of humankind. It is also a story of faith, courage, sacrifice and above all else, love.'

A Story of Towering Pride

Titanic really aspires to be not just a 'parable, a metaphor for the ills of humankind', but a 'story of faith and love', so it is certainly worth stopping to ask how such a movie compares with the Bible – the greatest story of faith and love, sacrifice and redemption. After all, Christians believe that the Bible is not only a 'story of faith', but *the* story. It may well pay to compare the story of the Titanic with the original script of the Bible.

Perhaps among the Bible's many narratives, the one that compares most closely to *Titanic* is the story of the Tower of Babel, which is found in its opening book, Genesis. With the same ambition of the *Titanic's* shipbuilders, the people of Babel decided to build a tremendous tower 'with it's top in the heavens'. The moral of the biblical story is that humanity had decided, with new-found technology, to try to usurp God's power. Seeing what was happening, God decided that such pride and arrogance could not go unpunished. The tower fell into ruin, and the proud people who tried to build it were 'scattered all over the face of the earth'.

I remember seeing a book illustration that helped you visualise the size of an ocean liner by standing it on end and comparing it to one of the world's tallest buildings.

The *Titanic* was a skyscraper at sea. It expressed both the technological prowess of its day and the pride and optimism of the people who built her. The owner, J. Bruce Ismay, is portrayed in the film as saying that he selected the name 'Titanic' to 'convey sheer size . . . and size means stability, luxury, and above all strength'.

The word 'Titanic' is derived from the word 'Titan', and the Titans were gigantic gods in Greek mythology. They were the twelve children of Uranus and Gaia – Heaven and Earth.

The *Titanic* was acclaimed for its great size and its seeming invincibility, and proclaimed to be the 'Ship of Dreams'.

Clip One: Setting Sail

It is the present day, and an elderly woman is talking directly to camera. She is reminiscing about the *Titanic*, 'the ship of dreams'. 'And it was. It really was,' she says, wistfully. The picture fades, and we see the bow end of the old boat, resting, rusting in its murky, blue watery grave. And the picture again fades, to replace the underwater image with a gleaming, pristine boat, sitting in Southampton dock on sunny day.

The harbour is a frenzy of busyness and excitement, as passengers get ready to board, and friends and family crowd to watch them. A shiny red Model-T Ford is winched onto the ship, as below, a line of cars draws up. From one of them steps a beautiful and clearly wealthy girl, together with her fiancé and her mother. It is Rose. She appears quite unmoved by the amazing sight that towers before her, observing sniffily that the Titanic doesn't even look as big as the Mauritania. 'Oh it is,' replies her fiancé, smugly, 'in fact, it's a hundred feet longer, and much more luxurious.'

Rose's mother surveys the scene with something approaching scepticism. 'So this is it', she says. 'This is the ship they say is unsinkable'. To which the man replies, proudly:

'God himself could not sink this ship.'

Flying in the Face of God

A survivor of the real *Titanic*, Eva Hart, recalled that her mother refused to go to sleep while aboard the maiden voyage, 'because she had this premonition, solely based on the fact that she said to declare a vessel unsinkable was flying in the face of God'. Of course, in the biblical story of the Tower of Babel, it is God, who brings the prideful building project to ruin. But for the people on board the *Titanic*, it's an encounter with an iceberg, which brings disaster upon them.

Premonitions and suspicions aside, the real enemies of the Titanic that fateful day were within. The decision was made by the ship's owners and captain to press on, at full speed, across the cold, dark waters of the North Atlantic, despite the fact that icebergs presented a very real danger. They were too preoccupied with the pride and prestige of achieving the fastest ever transatlantic crossing to worry that the ship might hit an iceberg and sink. After all, they had told the world that it was unsinkable, and unsinkable they believed it to be.

Although it's an iceberg that brings down the *Titanic*, God does have a role in the film – at least, he gets a mention. First, there is the music that is played just before the ship sinks. The band famously played on as the liner went down. Such hymns as 'Eternal Father, Strong to Save' and 'Nearer My God to Thee', became the soundtrack to an unimaginable disaster. God features, too, in the prayers and comments of those who turn in desperation to him for help. As the terrified passengers race to the highest point of the ship to escape the rising water, one reads from the Bible: 'Yea, though I walk through the valley of the shadow of death, I will fear no evil.' It's a comment to which Jack sarcastically asks, 'You want to walk a little faster through that valley?' Yet, the God implied by these appeals for mercy is one who does not intervene.

Clip Two: The Sinking

A seaman stands on deck, keeping watch through the night. He surveys the darkness before him through binoculars. Suddenly, he looks scared. There is a huge iceberg ahead, and it's too close for comfort – far too close. The *Titanic* has been set on 'full speed ahead' to break the transatlantic crossing record, despite the possibility of danger from icebergs. The seaman sends the message to the bridge: 'Iceberg! Iceberg!' It's passed frenetically on, and the officers send an order to the engine room.

The ship's huge iron engine shafts grind to a halt, and then crank the propeller into reverse. But it's too late, of course. The ship cannot turn in time, and hits the ice. Water cascades through the gash in the liner's side, while bodies cascade out. The ship's captain is woken, and enters the bridge. 'What was that?' he asks his colleague, Mr Murdoch. 'Iceberg,' comes the reply. The captain knows from Murdoch's expression that this is a fatal blow.

Elsewhere, as people begin to get the measure of what's happening, the lower class passengers are locked downstairs on their deck, so that those in first-class can get to the lifeboats. The violinist in a string quintet starts playing 'Nearer My God to Thee', and his colleagues, who were leaving, return, and join in. And as the music plays, the panic sets in around them.

The captain stands at the bridge, waiting, as the water rises. We see the designer of the *Titanic*, the man who dreamed this unsinkable vessel into being, standing in his luxurious quarters, realising that this ship is indeed sinkable after all. He checks his watch, and sets a clock on his mantelpiece. He knows that there is nothing he can do. Everywhere, people are scrambling, shouting, running, looking for lifeboats, as the water sweeps onto the upper deck. We see the captain for one last time, as the water pressure smashes the windows on the bridge, and the sea consumes him.

Outside, the water surrounds one of the glorious red funnels that were the hallmark of the liner. Its weight sends the huge tower crashing like a tree being felled, and it crushes all in its path as it falls. Meanwhile, in the mayhem, Jack has found Rose on deck. They have to stay on board for as long as possible, he says. The water is freezing, and it is filling up the lower decks, cascading through the ballroom and the opulent corridors of first class. It is tearing through the cages of the lower decks, where hundreds of men, women and children are trapped.

On the upper deck, a clergyman recites verses from the Bible: there will be no more sorrow or pain, he says, 'The old world has passed away.' Terrified passengers cling to his words – and to his hands. Suddenly, all the lights go out. And the whole scene is cast into an eerie, dark silence for a matter of seconds. It is the calm before the storm. Suddenly, the ship rips in two, or almost in two, as the first half sinks down headfirst. Bodies are flying everywhere, as the second half – still joined to the first at its bottom – is hoisted vertically by the downward force.

Jack and Rose have clambered to the bow of the liner, and cling on as it rises higher in the air, until it sits vertically, a colossal skyscraper in the sea that is about to descend into the depths forever. They hang on to the bars for dear life, as, like a rollercoaster ride, the second half of the ship begins to plummet. Jack shouts to Rose to take a deep, deep breath on his command, then to kick towards the surface, and keep kicking . . . and to hold his hand and never let go. 'This is it. Here we go!' The ship is disappearing into the water, and they are the last people to take the plunge. Jack screams to Rose: 'We're gonna make it, Rose. Trust me!' And at that, the waters close on the bow, forever – at the very spot where Rose and Jack had fallen in love.

The Folly of Human Arrogance

The question that this film raises in my mind is whether we, in the twenty-first century, have fallen into the same dreaming innocence as the passengers of that ill-fated ocean liner, who were dancing and dining while the 'ship of dreams' sailed toward destruction. They did not contemplate the fate that awaited them, either from the iceberg or from the terrible and tragic events that were threatening to unfold across Europe and the world after 1912. Confident in their wealth and technological prowess, and convinced that, should earthly treasures fail, a loving God would step in to rescue them, the ship carried on regardless.

Like them, we tend to forget about the past all too easily, and frequently ignore what the future seems to hold. Could our own ignorance carry us toward a similar fate today? Perhaps this hugely popular film will help to remind us of the folly of human arrogance, and sound a warning shot across our bows.

In 1898, fourteen years before the *Titanic* sank, the author Morgan Robertson wrote a novel, *Futility,* which told the story of a British ship called the *Titan.* It, like the *Titanic,* was on its maiden voyage from Britain to New York in the month of April with two thousand people on board. While it was attempting to cross the Atlantic in record time, it, too, struck an iceberg and sank. Most on board also died because, as with the *Titanic,* there were not enough lifeboats. Could this have been an amazing coincidence, or a prophetic parable?

The twentieth century was characterised as the age of ideology, the time of the 'isms': communism, socialism, Nazism, liberalism, humanism, scientism, and so on. Everywhere, such ideologies nurtured the idea that we humans could progress towards a better world without the help of God; they made us believe that we could bring about the ideal society, whether by revolution, racial genocide or scientific technology. Such an attitude is betrayed in *Titanic,* of course, when Rose's fiancé proudly boasts that 'even God himself could not sink her.'

But she did sink. And other idols have sunk, too. Nazism, of course, was forever disgraced by the horrors of its concentration camps and gas chambers. The Soviet Union and its dream of communism seemed to crumble, at least in the West, along with the Berlin Wall. Around the globe, socialist nations are ever more eager to establish 'free' economies. Even science, which for so long has been hailed as a saviour, threatens to behave like

Frankenstein's monster, which turned on its own creators. Most new discoveries and technologies can be used for good, but frequently they also threaten destruction.

Our Anchor in the Storms of Life

When we look at the past, all our major ideological constructions seem to have failed and been tossed onto the scrap heap of history. Only one compelling claim to the truth remains convincing. We still have one secure hope, one way of seeing and understanding our place in the world: Christianity. The church has lived through two millennia because its founder, Jesus Christ, remains the same – yesterday, today and forever.

On the fateful night of the *Titanic's* downfall, passengers who somehow still believed the hype, even refused to get in the lifeboats, despite being told that the ship was going down. They clung to their belief that the ship was unsinkable – and were actually offended when officers told them to evacuate, when they had paid such enormous sums of money for luxury accommodation. Other passengers were unable to get a place on the lifeboats because of the privileged few, who felt no concern for anyone but themselves. As a result, many of the boats, which were built to hold up to sixty people, left the *Titanic* with only fifteen aboard.

Through this film, the *Titanic* has been 'raised' for another generation of people to feel the impact of its tragic demise. It is an important warning against selfishness and arrogance, as well as a wonderfully positive affirmation of love, which transcends all lines of class, wealth and status.

Jesus Christ demonstrated the supreme act of love in human history, by dying on our behalf, and being raised from the dead.

If, as a race, we are sinking like the *Titanic,* then he has provided a lifeboat and we must all climb aboard. To miss it is to sink and die. Too many of us today continue to believe that the world is secure and safe, and that we're fine to press on, full-speed ahead into the darkness. But we need Jesus – and there is more than enough room for everyone at the Cross.

6

How Far Will You Go?

FARGO

Mark Stibbe

1996, Polygram
Directors: Joel & Ethan Coen
Starring: William H. Macy Steve Buscemi Frances McDormand Peter Stormare
Classification: 18

Temptation is an experience common to every human being so we should not be surprised to find that it's a frequent theme in the movies. Many films explore the destructive results of giving in to temptation. Temptation is therefore a very popular topic in film and in television. In fact, there is even a television show that's entirely devoted to this subject, called *Temptation Island*.

The film *Fargo* was written, produced and directed by the Coen brothers, Joel and Ethan, whose cinematic work is offbeat, but outstanding. *Fargo* is essentially a study in temptation. The Coen brothers claim that it's based on a true story of a kidnapping in Minnesota in 1987, though no one has been able to confirm that.

It is violent, but the violence serves a moral purpose, to highlight the appalling consequences of giving way to temptation.

The main character is Jerry Lundegaard (acted by William Macy). Jerry is a car salesman in Minneapolis. He is desperately insecure. He works for his rich, successful father-in-law, Wade Gustafson, who clearly dislikes him. He is married to a neurotic wife called Jean and has one son, called Scottie.

Jerry hires two incompetent criminals to kidnap his wife. His plan is to put up a ransom of $1,000,000 and to use the kidnappers to get the money from his father-in-law. In addition, he will rescue his wife, be a hero in her eyes, and pay off all his debts. He will pretend to the kidnappers that the ransom is only $80,000 and give half to them. This is his plan.

Where Temptation Starts

The Bible talks a lot about the phenomenon of temptation. In the book of James we read: 'When tempted, no-one should say, "God is tempting me." For God cannot be tempted by evil, nor does he tempt anyone; but each one is tempted when, by his own evil desire, he is dragged away and enticed. Then, after desire has conceived, it gives birth to sin; and sin, when it is full-grown, gives birth to death' (James 1:13–15). Here James describes temptation as a process involving three stages: (1) the desire for something destructive leads to (2) sinful or selfish actions, and these in turn lead to (3) one's own death, the death of relationships, and so on.

Jerry Lundegaard is a man who succumbs to temptation. He is driven by a need to succeed. He believes that success will earn him the respect and admiration of his wife and his wife's father. In order to fulfil his false dream, Jerry falls for the commonest desire of all, the love of money, which the Bible says is the root of all evil.

Clip One: The Plot is Hatched

In the opening scene of the film, Jerry drives into a small town in mid-winter. The snow is falling. He enters the bar. In contrast to the classic Western saloon scene, no one even turns to look at Jerry as he enters. The music goes on playing and the people continue to talk. Jerry sits down with two men who turn out to be the villains of the film, Carl Showalter (Steve Buscemi) and Gaear Grimsrod (Peter Stormare). In the dialogue that follows, Jerry enlists the help of these two foul-mouthed characters to initiate the plan to kidnap his wife, though even these two criminals express surprise at the depravity of this plan:

CARL: You want your own wife kidnapped?
JERRY: The thing is, my wife, she's wealthy. Her dad, he's real well off. Now, I'm in a bit of trouble . . .
CARL: What kind of trouble you in, Jerry?
JERRY: Well . . . that's . . . I'm not going to get into that. . . . See . . . I need the money. See, her dad, he's real well off.
CARL: So why don't you ask him for the money?
JERRY: Well . . . they don't know I need it. See, okay, there's that. And even if they did, I wouldn't get it. So there's that . . .

In spite of the insane and irrational nature of the plan, the two crooks agree to take on what they call the 'mission' and a catastrophic chain of events is begun.

Desire has been conceived. Sin is about to be born.

Rita Mae Brown once said: 'Lead me not into temptation, I can find the way myself'. That is exactly what Jerry does. He finds the way himself. He runs into temptation with the relentless, irrational dive of a lemming. He is totally enticed by the thought of something forbidden. Roman poet and historian Tacitus said that 'forbidden things have a secret charm'. Jerry discovers that early on in the movie. He is enchanted by the very thing that will bring about his ruin. This is always where temptation starts. It starts with 'the fascination of the forbidden'. It begins with desiring that which will ultimately destroy who we are and what we value. Many films express the perverse illogic of this self-destructive tendency in our human nature. *Fargo* is perhaps the most disturbing and yet the most interesting of all recent movies on this theme.

Where Temptation Leads

Let's go back to our passage from the Book of James. James says that 'each one is tempted when, by his own evil desire, he is dragged away and enticed. Then, after desire has conceived, it gives birth to sin; and sin, when it is full-grown, gives birth to death'. Remember, the Bible is a very practical book. It deals with real-life issues. Here James tells us exactly what every human being can expect if they embark on the process of giving way to temptation. They can expect entanglement to follow enticement, and entrapment to follow entanglement.

The end of the road, says James, is death.

This is exactly the story of Jerry Lundegaard. The actions initiated by Jerry's desire are truly terrifying. The two goons kidnap Jerry's wife, but they are stopped for driving without number plates on a remote road. They shoot the State trooper who pulls them over, as well as a young couple who just happen to be driving by. They end up killing Jerry's father-in-law, and a car park attendant, before finally killing Jerry's wife. Then, one of the kidnappers – Gaear – turns on his accomplice and kills him. He is finally arrested, and so is Jerry, who is hiding out in a dingy motel room.

Clip Two: Assessing the Mayhem

The effects of Jerry saying 'yes' to temptation are vividly and brutally presented in the film. We have a chance to reflect on the carnage when two police officers are at the scene of the first killings. They are drinking coffee and chatting about everyday life. A car lies on its back in the snow beside the state freeway. A young couple lie hidden from our view inside. Both of them have been shot dead. A state trooper lies about fifty yards away, his blood starkly contrasting with the whiteness of the snow. The chief of police approaches the state trooper's body and examines it, perfectly reconstructing the trail of destruction through the footprints and other clues. She correctly realises that this is 'an execution-type deal' and says of the state trooper, 'Looks like a nice guy. It's a real shame'. She then gets into her police car with Lou, the other officer, and returns to town discussing number plates.

The portrayal of the actual killing of these three people, not to mention this subsequent examination of the crime scene, is graphic. The viewer should be warned. But the Coen brothers are not being gratuitous in their depiction of the chaos that emerges from Jerry's plan. The graphic violence serves to underline the base and bestial depravity that human beings will sink to when temptation overpowers just one person. Ordinary people with 'decent' lives can self-destruct with spectacular pathos under the alluring and seductive power of temptation. In a movie called *Fargo*, the Coen brothers have come up with a story that vividly and despairingly illustrates how far we will go when tempted. Temptation leads towards a dark horizon, just like the freeways in *Fargo*.

Where Temptation Ends

Back to James 1:15, 'After desire has conceived, it gives birth to sin; and sin, when it is full-grown, gives birth to death'. Temptation ends in death. This is the case for Jerry Lundegaard. His sinful deeds led to the death of many people and to personal disaster. He loses absolutely everything, even his dignity. Indeed, when he is finally captured, he is arrested in his underpants; screaming and whining like a trapped animal. This final glimpse of Jerry, supercharged with bathos, serves to act as a reminder to everyone that temptation involves a road to self-destruction. It involves everything being stripped away. The moral message is 'do not succumb to temptation'. Do not allow sinful desires to lead you astray. Terminate them at conception. Otherwise, it will all end in tears.

One of the ways in which this point is highlighted is through the Coen brothers' brilliant creation of the character, Marge Gunderson (acted by Oscar winner, Frances McDormand – Joel Coen's wife). Marge is the female police chief who follows the trail of destruction in the movie. She is heavily pregnant and cannot stop eating. We first see her asleep in bed with her devoted husband Norm (i.e. 'Normal') who seems to spend the entire film either cooking or eating. During his first words in the film he says 'I'll fix you some eggs' three times! Their marriage is portrayed as decent, simple, and orderly, befitting the Scandinavian ancestry their surname suggests.

Clip Three: The Diner with Mike

Marge also experiences temptation in the film, when an old school friend called Mike rings her. Marge accepts an invitation to a meal, dresses in a flowery dress, dons an unusual amount of make-up, and enters the restaurant.

Marge sits opposite him and they exchange pleasantries. She asks Mike about his marriage and, before he answers, he moves over to the other side of the table sitting very close to Marge. As he sits he asks, 'Do you mind if I sit over here?' Marge looks away and without hesitation says emphatically, 'No, why don't you sit over there? I prefer that'. Mike moves back saying, 'Ok, sorry'. He then invents a pathetic story about his wife Linda's death (which turns out in fact to be a lie). 'I've been so lonely', he sobs.

The difference between Marge and Jerry is superbly highlighted throughout this scene. On the one hand, Jerry falls for temptation. A sinful desire is conceived in his heart and, at a restaurant table, he initiates a disastrous sequence of events. Marge, on the other hand, terminates temptation at conception. Her very definite act of resistance (also at a restaurant table) offers the clearest contrast to Jerry's lack of resistance. These two characters show that there are really two places temptation can end. Either we succumb to temptation and have it all end in destruction (Jerry), or we can end the whole ugly process before it is even born (Marge).

While Marge is depicted as a moral being, Jerry is depicted as an immoral being. While Marge represents the triumph of decency, Jerry represents the tragedy of indecency. The contrast between them is as black and white as the landscapes they inhabit.

> All the water in the world, however hard it tries
> Can never sink the smallest ship unless it gets inside
> And all the evil in the world, the blackest kind of sin
> Can never hurt you in the least unless you let it in.

Asking God for Help

A much-loved man who attended our church, Dave Harding, died in 1998. Shortly before he died, Dave gave an amazing testimony about how God had miraculously set him free from alcohol addiction. The following is a transcript taken from the tape.

Before 1997 my life was a real shambles, totally unmanageable and totally dominated by alcohol – supplemented, when possible, with drugs. It is difficult to explain how all-pervasive it was. Doctors would ask me what time of the day I started drinking. That was a completely ridiculous question. If I woke at three in the morning, I would start. If I woke at three in the afternoon, I would start. It just dominated all my actions and all my thoughts.

Since the age of 20 – I am 50 now – I have tried various means of stopping. I have been in and out of hospitals, clinics, treatment centres, and various types of therapy and counselling. I was frequently warned that my liver was going bad.

In the end, something happened on Boxing Day 1997. I had my last drink on 26 December. I then started experiencing DTs and it was absolute dreadful. I honestly thought I was going to die that night, but in that place of despair, I prayed. I think for the first time in my life I was utterly defeated I knew no power on earth could help me and there was only one possible way out. That was to pray to the Lord to help me through that night and to take away the desire I had for alcohol. That's where it all starts, with desire.

A sort of peace came over me and I had this hope that life did not have to be as it had been. I was completely alone except for the Lord, and I asked him in to my life and he came and he answered my prayer.

I used to pray in a rather insincere fashion. I'd pray in the morning with a drink in my hand asking that I might not drink

> too much that day. But when I prayed for myself on 26 December, this time I was sincere. That night, Jesus came in to my heart.
>
> Strange as it sounds since Boxing Day 1997, I have not had a single desire to drink and that is a miracle. The consultant I was under said it was very unusual in his experience for someone of my age and history of drinking to manage to stop just like that. I told him it came from the Lord, and he suggested I should stick with that.

Not long after that, Dave Harding died. But when J. John and I visited him on the evening of his death, we met a man who had conquered his addiction and was at peace with God. Dave Harding was a man who had known the destructive power of temptation. When he asked Jesus into his heart, he experienced a miracle. God took away the desire for alcohol. God can do that with our temptations too. He can take the desire, if we ask.

A Movie with a Message

Fargo is like a post-modern morality tale. It is a very stark reminder of the dangers of giving in to any temptation, but particularly the temptation of money. Just before the movie finishes, Marge is sitting in a police car with the surviving villain in the back, behind a cage. She speaks to him as she looks at his reflection in the mirror. The man remains silent. 'And for what?' she asks. 'For a little bit of money. There's more to life than a little money, you know. Don't you know that? And here you are. And it's a beautiful day. Well, I just don't understand'. At this point, the haunting music score of Carter Burwell kicks in and the scene moves to the motel of Jerry's arrest.

Marge's lament at the end of this film is so poignant. There really is more to life than money, yet so many peoples' lives are destroyed by the temptation of financial greed. Other people, like Dave Harding, experience different kinds of temptation. However, it is probably right to say that the most common is the love of money. As the Apostle Paul wrote, in his first letter to Timothy, 'People who want to get rich fall into temptation and a trap and into many foolish and harmful desires that plunge men into ruin and destruction. For the love of money is a root of all kinds of evil' (1 Timothy 6:9–10). It is so sad that many of us fail to heed the warning.

I conclude with a true and tragic example of how – in the process of temptation – desire leads to sinful actions, and sinful actions end in death.

In November 2001, a 28-year-old Japanese woman called Tukako Konishi was found wandering around at a landfill and truck stop in Bismarck, North Dakota. A man found her and took her to the police station where she showed officers a crude map of a tree next to a highway. She believed that this was the place where Carl Showalter had buried the kidnapper's ransom in the movie *Fargo*, and she was trying to find it.

The police tried to persuade her that *Fargo* was just a movie (though there really is a place called Fargo in North Dakota), but the woman insisted that the film had been based on a true story, therefore the treasure must be buried somewhere. The Bismarck police tried in vain to convince her that the movie was fictional, not factual, but to no avail. Miss Konishi left the police station, boarded a bus, and went to Fargo.

A few days later, a hunter stumbled across her body in a grove of pine trees in Detroit Lakes. She had taken some sedatives, but the cause of death was put down as exposure. Her death was eventually ruled a suicide when it was discovered that she had sent a letter to her family in Japan expressing her intention to take her own life.

7

TIME AND ETERNITY

CAST AWAY

J. John

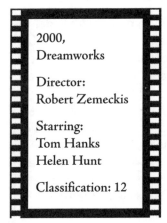

2000,
Dreamworks

Director:
Robert Zemeckis

Starring:
Tom Hanks
Helen Hunt

Classification: 12

I remember day-dreaming in a boring lecture at theological college one day, when the lecturer stopped and asked, 'Mr John, will you tell me why you keep looking at your watch?' I had to think quickly. 'Yes, sir,' I said. 'I was concerned that you might not have time to finish your interesting lecture.'

Someone who perhaps paid a little more attention in their classes, Albert Einstein, once said, 'When a man sits with a pretty girl for an hour, it seems like a minute. But let him sit on a hot stove for a minute and it's longer than any hour. That's relativity.' Time plays a significant role in our lives, and we can't ever seem to shake it off.

In *Cast Away*, Tom Hanks plays Chuck Noland, a manic Federal Express trouble-shooter who travels the world at a moment's notice. Both his professional and personal life are ruled by the clock, and the words, 'time', 'watch' and 'pager' are spoken of twenty-four times in the first fifteen minutes. Early in the film, Noland, a man seemingly in control of everything, gives a speech on the theme of time to a group of Russian Federal Express employees.

Clip One: The Speaking Clock

A boy runs over a bridge, clutching a parcel with Federal Express labels on it. It's snowy and cold. He keeps running. We cut to the scene inside what looks like a warehouse, where Chuck Noland is lecturing Russian Federal Express employees on the virtues of timekeeping. It's all a battle against the relentless march of time, he argues passionately. Clocks tick away as his visual aid to people of another country, another culture, for whom this idea seems a little foreign. A Russian translator keeps up with his increasingly frenetic exhortations to 'keep time'.

Suddenly, he notices that the boy with the parcel is before him, panting. He grabs it, and opens it. 'What could it be?' he asks, patronisingly. His tone prompts sarcasm from the translator, who says something he can't understand.

Pulling out the contents, it's … another clock, a stopwatch, in fact, that he sent to himself by Federal Express and which he started the moment he left Memphis for Russia. It has taken eighty-seven hours, twenty-two minutes and seventeen seconds for the package to arrive.

Too long! It's just not good enough!

What if the parcel had been something really important?

Noland then turns to the job in hand: the Russians have a pile of packages that must be gathered and loaded onto a truck in under fifteen minutes to be sent to the airport. 'It's crunch time,' he declares. 'Let's go!'

If Only there was Enough Time

I'm sure you'd agree that the pace of life is hectic. We talk of the 'peak' or 'rush' hour. We are always telling our children to 'hurry up, get a move on!' It is because our days are too full and because they move too fast that we never seem to catch up with ourselves. Our work and the demands upon us seem to expand to fit all the time that we have. Time is increasingly in short supply. And we spend a good deal of our time complaining about it.

How often have you heard yourself, or others say, 'If only I had the time'? Or, 'There's never enough time.' 'I don't know where the time goes.' 'But how do you find the time?' 'I'm hard pressed for time at present.' 'I'll try to find time.' 'Is that the time already?' 'My, how time flies!' 'Could you fit in time?' 'I'm short of time.' 'Mustn't waste time, must we?' 'I just ran out of time.' 'I don't even get time to think.'

We have a wide range of other expressions as well: 'I haven't got a moment to spare.' 'There are never enough hours in the day.' 'We always seem to be on the go.' 'There's always so much to do.' 'I never seem to stop.' 'We're flat out at the moment.' 'I've just got to rush.' 'The week's simply flown.' 'Back to the treadmill.' 'No rest for the wicked.' Then, there's the revealing invitation: 'You must come around some time . . .'

The pace of many people's lives is literally killing them. We have bought into the crazy idea that the busier we are, the more important our life is. We live in a society in which the expression 'time is money' has come to refer to the value of time. The only problem with this is that money cannot buy more time. We forget that money can be replaced, but time can never be replaced. We would be far richer as individuals and as a society if we were to say that 'time is priceless'. Then we might treat it with more respect.

Our modern hustle and bustle places us in the grip of what the psychologist Paul Tournier calls 'universal fatigue'. People are constantly complaining about how tired they feel. We even feel tired when we wake up in the morning. Diane Fassel wrote in her book *Working Ourselves to Death* that 'work is god for the compulsive worker, and nothing gets in the way of this god.' Work becomes an end in itself, a way to escape from family, from the inner life, from the world.

When Time Stands Still

Following his speech in Russia, Chuck flies back to Memphis to see his long-time girlfriend Kelly (played by Helen Hunt), the girl he's about to propose to. But Chuck lives in such bondage to time that he can't even schedule time for a dental appointment. During a Christmas dinner, his pager goes off. He is called immediately to South East Asia to deal with another Federal Express problem. He and Kelly hurriedly open their Christmas gifts to each other in the car, on the way to the airport. Chuck gives Kelly a journal and a pager in order to record her life in the world of time. She gives him a pocket watch – a family heirloom, in fact – with her picture inside.

He says, 'I will keep it on Memphis time – Kelly time.' He then hands her a ring box with the parting words, 'I'll be right back.'

Halfway over the Pacific Ocean, his plane is brought down by a terrible storm. Chuck is the only survivor. Somehow, he reaches shore on a small deserted island. The first thing Chuck removes is his pager, which is filled with water, and then his pocket watch, which has stopped.

Time as he knew it has ended. The clock is no longer a pulsating, relentless taskmaster. Having lived his life by the second hand, Chuck realises that time is not under his control any more than the circumstances of his existence. This awareness forces him to face the self-imposed limitations of his life. Chuck tried to measure everything with time, but didn't know how to use it. He abused and ignored people. He now gets pushed outside time – cast away. The maddening thing for him is that while his own clock may have stopped, the world's time marches on.

So, we have a man obsessed with time who is trapped in a purgatory that he cannot regulate. He goes from clocking seconds digitally to tracking the seasons by the movement of the sun. He no longer controls time – it controls him. In a touching scene he looks at the ID of one of the dead crewmen who was washed ashore, just before burying him – and realises that he didn't even know his real name. It is a moving testimony to the tyranny of the urgent and how busyness can distract us from relating to the people who are close to us at a deeper level.

We then see how Chuck figures out the four basic elements for human survival: food, water, shelter and fire. But there is a fifth element he needs badly – companionship. Federal Express packages from the plane crash begin to wash ashore – packages he can't deliver. Chuck finds novel uses for their contents, but decides not to open one particular parcel that is adorned with angel wings. The wings become a symbol of hope for him, one that far outweighs any physical use he could have found for what was inside.

In one of the boxes, he finds a volleyball. Having cut his hand, and then grabbing the volleyball, his bloodstain leaves an image of a strangely compelling face. With slight modifications of his own, Chuck uses his own blood not only to create, but also to bond with his new companion. 'Wilson' becomes the 'friend' who keeps Chuck sane while he's on the edge.

Only after four years does Chuck make a daring – and successful – escape from the island. He returns to civilisation a profoundly changed human being, but realises that he can't pick up where he left off. On the plane flying home, his friend Stan tells Chuck they held a funeral for him. They put in his coffin a phone, beeper and Elvis CDs – which they had decided were the things that best represented his life.

Clip Two: All the Time in the World

Noland is sat in a house, in semi-darkness, talking to his friend. He has a drink in his hand, and is reflective. He tells of how he talked to Kelly when he was on the island; that even though he was totally alone, she was with him. He knew, or thought he knew, that he would get ill, or injured, and die. Everything had been out of his control . . . apart from one thing: his own death. The only choice he had, the one thing he could determine, was how and when and where it would happen. So, he'd made a rope, and climbed a hill to hang himself. He tested the rope first, to see if it would bear his weight, but the log he used snapped the branch on which the rope hung. He realised that he didn't have power over anything. He couldn't even kill himself properly! But all of a sudden, he said, a feeling came over him – like a warm blanket. He knew, somehow, that he had to stay alive, keep breathing – even though there was no reason to hope, and even though he didn't believe that he would ever see this room again – so that's what he did. And the tide came in, and washed up a sail . . . and here he is, talking to his friend, in Memphis.

But after all that . . . after everything . . . after his hope in the face of despair . . . he's lost Kelly again. And he's desperately sad about it. But, in the face of that sadness, he can remain happy that she was somehow with him on the island. And now? He's got to keep breathing, once more. Tomorrow, he says, the sun will rise. And who knows what that could bring?

The Absence of God

Cast Away, to use a quote from the Berlioz requiem, is 'haunted by the absence of God'. In contrast, Daniel Defoe's seventeenth-century novel *Robinson Crusoe* is filled with God's presence. Crusoe is a man who rebels against his parents to become a sailor. He joins up with a ship to set out for the Seven Seas in search of adventure.

He becomes the sole survivor of a shipwreck, condemned to live out his days on a desert island. Though Chuck Noland and Robinson Crusoe experience similar circumstances – both being stranded on a desert island – Crusoe, in direct contrast, begins to contemplate time and eternity.

The book *Robinson Crusoe* is full of his thoughtful, probing encounters with God – his weaknesses, fears, temptations. It explores how Crusoe learns to love God and the world. He is someone who runs from God and who cries out to God. And this is what's disappointing about *Cast Away*. In the end, the film only offers a picture of the person that seems far away from the reality of human experience. Crusoe's pilgrimage rings true in a way that *Cast Away* simply does not.

Noland stressed three points in his speech at the beginning of the film in Russia. First, he states that time rules over us without mercy. Christians might disagree, and argue that it is God who rules with mercy. Second, he says that we live and die by the clock – rather than by the grace of a sovereign God. Third, he says, never turn your back on the clock or commit the sin of losing track of time – it is a pulsating, relentless taskmaster. But he has no concept of a loving, compassionate God.

The psalmist writes, 'Our days on earth are like grass; like wildflowers, we bloom and die. The wind blows, and we are gone – as though we had never been here. But the love of the Lord remains forever with those who fear him. His salvation extends to the children's children of those who are faithful to his covenant, of those who obey his commandments' (Psalm 103:15–18). The writer of Ecclesiastes states beautifully that 'God has placed eternity in our hearts.' And because God has placed 'eternity in our hearts', we know that nothing of 'time' will permanently satisfy us.

One thing we can observe from films like *Cast Away* is the utter emptiness of life without God. Life derives its true meaning not from self-fulfilment or success, but from a personal relationship with our creator. As C. S. Lewis once said, 'If I find in myself a desire which no experience in this world can satisfy, the most probable explanation is that I was made for another world.'

When God Intervenes

There is a story in the life of Jesus, recorded in John 5:2–9. 'Inside the city, near the Sheep Gate, was the pool of Bethesda, with five covered porches. Crowds of sick people – blind, lame or paralysed – lay on the porches. One of the men lying there had been sick for thirty-eight years. When Jesus saw him and knew how long he had been ill, he asked him, "Would you like to get well?"

' "I can't, sir," the sick man said, "for I have no one to help me into the pool when the water is stirred up. While I am trying to get there, someone else always gets in ahead of me."

'Jesus told him, "Stand up, pick up your sleeping mat, and walk!"

'Instantly, the man was healed! He rolled up the mat and began walking.'

The man had been lying there for thirty-eight years, his eyes staring at the water; his gaze fixed on his only hope of something better. The very cause of his need prevented him from having that need met. Suddenly, his world is interrupted by a voice asking him if he wants to be made well. What a strange question! Surely, the answer is obvious? But his answer is revealing: it's not 'Yes, that's what I've been longing for,' but a statement of the problem as he sees it – he has no one to help him into the pool.

Originally, all he wanted was to be healed, to walk and run as others could. Now, all he wants is someone to help him in to the water. The pool has become the object of his longing, and he cannot see any other solution to his problem. Sometimes, the search, however wearying and unfulfilled, becomes everything for us.

In fact, all he needed was a word from Jesus and, in an instant the pool, which had been his hope and his despair for thirty-eight years, seemed unimportant.

No matter how hard we try, we cannot pull ourselves out of the quicksand of time. That is why we need someone to change the way we see things, to lift our eyes, so that we can peer beyond time and be led towards eternity. That someone is Jesus. Our search for eternity brings us to him. Jesus said, 'I am the way, the truth and the life.' Life with Christ is an endless hope; without him, it is a hopeless end.

At the Crossroads of Life

In the movie *The Last Emperor*, the young child anointed as the last Emperor of China lives a life of luxury with a thousand servants at his command. 'What happens when you do wrong?' his brother asks. 'When I do wrong, someone else is punished,' the boy replies. To demonstrate, he breaks a jar, and one of his servants is beaten.

In Christianity, Jesus reversed that ancient pattern: when the servants erred, the King was punished. Grace was free only because the giver himself bore the cost.

At the end of *Cast Away*, we see Chuck Noland standing at a crossroads. He is in the middle of the road, able to go in any one of four different directions.

Clip Three: At the Crossroads

Chuck Noland parks at a sweeping crossroads, in the middle of, well, seemingly nowhere. One road seems white, sandy, yet the others are dark. It's a hot day, and the sky is blue. The landscape is flat and yields no clues about direction. He gets out of his car and unfolds a map. Another car swings by and stops. A woman, happy, smiling, helpful, tells him he looks lost. 'Where you headed?' she asks. That was what he was trying to figure out, he replies. She tells him exactly where each road leads, which directions he can choose. And with that, briefly, she wishes him luck, and drives off, up the white path – her dog peering at him from the back of her pickup. Chuck stands there, watching her drive into the distance. He looks round at every path, slowly. And stares once more along the woman's path.

> The road Noland was standing on was in the light, but the other three were in the dark. The movie's final scene ends with Chuck seeing the wings on the woman's truck.

Making Time for What Really Matters

In St Paul's Cathedral in London hangs Holman Hunt's painting, *The Light of the World*. It is a picture of a cottage that is run down, and bushes and briars have grown around it. The path is covered by weeds and grass. Standing at the door, Jesus is holding a lantern in one hand that gives off light to every part of the picture, and he is knocking with the other hand. After Hunt completed the picture, one discerning critic said to him, 'Mr Hunt, you made a mistake. There is no handle on the door.' The artist replied, 'No, I did not make a mistake, for there is a handle. The handle is on the inside.'

Once a little girl and her father were standing in the cathedral. They were mesmerised as they looked at the painting. Then the girl asked, 'Daddy, did they ever let him in?'

A few years ago, I had a dialogue with an atheist professor. He spent a good deal of time mocking both Christ and my experience of him. In front of me was a fruit bowl, and I ate a tangerine. After I had finished, I asked the professor, 'Was the tangerine sweet or sour?' He said, 'How can I know whether it was sweet or sour when I never tasted it?' And I replied, 'And how can you know anything about Christ if you have not tried him?'

God our Father is the maker of everything that exists. He is the Author of the world of nature, and the Creator of both space and time. Without God, there would be no past, present or future: no summer or winter, spring or autumn, seedtime or harvest. There would be no morning or evening, or months or years. Because God gives us the gift of time, we have the opportunity to think and to act; to plan and to pray; to give and to receive; to create and to relate; to work and to rest; to strive and to play; to love and to worship. Too often, we forget this, and we fail to appreciate God's generosity. We take time for granted and fail to thank God for it. We view it as a commodity and ruthlessly exploit it. We cram it too full, waste it, learn too little from the past, or mortgage it off in advance.

In doing so, we also refuse to give priority to those people and things which should have chief claim upon our time. We need God's help to view time as he sees it, and to use it more as he intends. It is crucial to try to distinguish between what is central and what is peripheral; between what is really pressing, and what can wait; between what is our responsibility and what can be left to others; and between what is appropriate now and what will be more relevant later.

We need God to help guard us against attempting too much, because of our false sense of our indispensability, our false sense of ambition, our false sense of rivalry, of guilt and inferiority.

We also need God to help us not to mistake our responsibilities, underestimate ourselves, or overlook our weaknesses and to understand our proper limits. We need to realise that, important though this life is, it is not *all* that there is. So, we should view everything we do in the light of eternity, not just our limited horizons. It is a matter of true perspective.

God is not so much timeless, as timeful. He does not live above time so much as hold all times together. Despite its inadequacies, the film *Cast Away* is, above all, a timely reminder.

8

The Truth Shall Set You Free!

THE MATRIX

Mark Stibbe

1998, Warner Bros.

Directors: Andy & Larry Wachowski

Starring:
Keanu Reeves
Lawrence Fishburne
Carrie-Anne Moss
Hugo Wearing

Classification: 15

The Matrix is one of the most exciting as well as thought-provoking science fiction pictures ever made. There are few films more stylish, insightful, and groundbreaking in terms of special effects (e.g. the invention of 'bullet time'). Written and directed by the Wachowski brothers, produced by Joel Silver, and starring Keanu Reeves, *The Matrix* quite simply redefines the word 'cool'.

The Matrix is the story of Neo Anderson, who discovers that the world he lives in is, in reality, a computer-generated world designed to deceive and enslave humanity. Only a few know the truth: a man called Morpheus and a woman called Trinity, plus their small band of rebels. Their ship, the *Nebuchadnezzar*, travels from the one remaining city on earth that has not been enslaved – a city called Zion, near the earth's core. They search for the chosen one who will rescue humanity from their slavery and they find Anderson, believing he's the one.

If ever there was a film that invited a spiritual interpretation, it's this one. In fact, you could approach it from a number of faith perspectives. You could examine it from a Buddhist perspective (the world as illusion). You could study it from a Jewish perspective (Neo as a liberator like Moses, a deliverer of people from bondage). There are many different ways you can look at this film, but perhaps the most obvious is a Christian one. The name of the ship, the *Nebuchadnezzar*, is the name of an Old Testament Babylonian king. The name of the city, Zion, is one that you can find in both the Old and the New Testaments of the Bible. The name 'Trinity' is overtly Christian: it is the technical term describing the Christian's unique understanding of God as three in one.

Then of course, there is Neo himself. There are very strong parallels between Neo and the Messiah of the Bible. Neo means 'new' in Greek. 'Ander' means 'man', so 'Anderson' could be transliterated as 'son of man', making 'Neo Anderson' 'new son of man'. When you consider that 'Son of Man' was Jesus' preferred way of describing himself in the Gospels, this is obviously significant. Neo Anderson, who dies and is resurrected in the movie, is an obvious Christ figure in modern cinema.

As in the Gospels, the central theme of the film really comprises bad news and good news. The bad news is the truth that we are slaves and we don't realise it. The good news is that freedom has been made possible through sacrifice. This is the central theme of *The Matrix* and it's the central theme of the

New Testament. The New Testament story tells of a world enslaved by the devil, with every human being unwittingly born into slavery to sin. But Jesus came in to this enslaved world to awaken us to our true situation. He came to die a sacrificial death in order that we might be set free from sin.

As Jesus said to those who would follow him: 'You will know the truth, and the truth will set you free' (John 8:32)

How Much do You Know?

The Matrix is a great parable of our spiritual condition, as described in the Bible. This film encourages us to look very carefully at ourselves and to ask three basic questions about our lives. First: How much do we know? Second: What is the truth? Third: How can we be set free? In what follows, let's look at how the Bible answers these questions, and how *The Matrix* answers them too.

So, first of all, how much do you really know? Dee Hock, the visionary leader of VISA, said this: 'The problem is never how to get new, imaginative thoughts into your mind, but how to get the old ones out. Every mind is a room packed with archaic furniture. You must get the old furniture of what you know, think and believe, out before anything new can get in. Make an empty space in any corner of your mind and creativity will instantly fill it.'

The clear message of the Bible is this: our minds are basically full of darkness. Until we have experienced the illumination of God's Spirit, we are portrayed in the New Testament as ignorant, blind and asleep. Our thinking is described as futile and our understanding as darkened. We do not live God-centred, but self-centred lives. Consequently, our minds are full of confusion and deception, not clarity and truth. As the Apostle Paul put it, 'The god of this age has blinded the minds of unbelievers, so that they cannot see the light of the gospel of the glory of Christ, who is the image of God' (2 Corinthians 4:4).

You couldn't get a clearer or more damning diagnosis than that. We are not enlightened, according to the Bible. We may be knowledgeable scientifically, but we are not knowledgeable spiritually. We are slaves to sin, and our minds are therefore asleep. The only answer according to the Bible is to choose to turn from an old way of thinking to a new way of thinking, to empty our minds of the old furniture of what we know, and to make space for the light of God's truth. The Bible calls this repentance: making a U-turn from a sinful to a godly life. This kind of repentance is a human choice. It is the most vital decision we make.

Clip One: Making the Right Choice

About half an hour into the movie, Neo Anderson is beginning to realise that something is badly wrong with the world. He meets up with a woman called Trinity who takes him to see Morpheus. She takes him to a door and says, 'This is it. Let me give you one piece of advice. Be honest: he knows more than you can imagine'.

Neo enters and sits opposite Morpheus. The room is dark, the clothing is black, but the armchairs are red. 'You have the look of a man who accepts what he sees because he is expecting to wake up', Morpheus says. 'Ironically, this is not far from the truth.'

Morpheus continues to explain why Neo has come to see him. 'You are here because you know something. What you know you can't explain but you feel it. You've felt it your entire life, that there's something wrong with the world. You don't know what it is, but it's there, like a splinter in your mind'.

Morpheus challenges Neo, 'Do you know what I'm talking about?' Neo answers correctly, 'The Matrix'. Morpheus asks, 'Do you want to know what it is?' Neo nods and Morpheus explains that the Matrix is all around them, it is the world of illusion that has been designed to blind people from the truth. When Neo asks, 'What truth?' Morpheus replies, 'The truth that that you are a slave, Neo. Like everyone else you were born into bondage . . . into a prison for your mind'.

Morpheus concludes that no one can be told about the Matrix. They have to see it for themselves. He then offers Neo a last chance to make a decision. He offers Neo a choice between a blue pill, which will enable Neo to forget the conversation, and to wake up in his bed oblivious to everything, and a red pill, the path to seeing the truth. 'Remember', he says, 'all I'm offering is the truth. Nothing more'.

As Neo takes the red pill, Morpheus says, 'Follow me'. Neo then begins his journey of enlightenment.

What a picture this is of our spiritual condition without God. We know deep down that this life is not all there is to human existence. We sense that there must be more. As Morpheus puts it, you can feel it when you go out to work, or go to church. You just know that there's more to know than you know. It's like an itch on your soul.

Benjamin Disraeli once said, 'To be conscious that you are ignorant is a great step to knowledge'.

Jesus said, 'You shall know the truth'. So how much do you know?

What is the Truth?

We are told in society today that there is no absolute truth. All truth is relative; it is subjective; you construct your own reality.

Recently I was speaking to someone whose husband is receiving counselling. Their marriage is suffering, and it's looking as though they are going to end up getting divorced. One reason why there is no reconciliation in this situation is because the counsellor is encouraging the husband to construct his own reality. He is being told, 'If that's what you perceive happened, then that's what happened'.

Personally, I think this is incredibly dangerous advice. It does not help people to face reality. It does not help people to change with any degree of depth and integrity. True transformation only comes when you see the truth, when you move from subjective perception to objective reality. It's only when you see things as they really are that you can be free.

Let me give you a personal example. Shortly after our birth, my twin sister and I were placed by our mother in an orphanage in Hackney, North London. For much of my life my perception of my birth mother has been, accordingly, very negative. This affected my relationship with my adoptive mother and my relationship with women generally.

However, a year ago I was watching a production in a theatre in London. A friend of mine, Brian Doerksen, wrote a musical called *The Father's House,* a theatrical parable about our relationship with God as our Father. He had asked a few of his friends to see a preview and comment on it before it went on general release. I duly went, not expecting anything other than a time of constructively critiquing Brian's work.

However, there was a scene in this musical when a young mother was agonising about giving up her child for adoption. This single mother was weeping over the prospect. She wasn't doing it callously. To express her pain, she sang a poignant, heart-rending song. Suddenly I found myself crying. All those years thinking that my birth mother had been uncaring melted away. I began to understand the pain that she, as a single mother, must have gone through. I began to see her from a more truthful perspective.

A few months later my adoptive mother sent me a letter that she had received from my birth mother after I had been adopted. The letter is the only thing I have from my biological mother and it expresses how she felt when she gave my sister and me up for adoption. There were a couple of lines in it which gave the clearest indication that she had agonised over the decision and found it very hard to let us go. She hadn't cruelly abandoned us, as I had assumed, but had given us up only as the last resort. As I reflected on this, I saw that my perception of reality and reality itself were two different things. I had perceived my mother to be heartless, and all my life I'd had this very negative impression of mothers. Now I saw things very differently. I saw the truth, and the truth set me free from years of bitterness and unforgiveness. Jesus said, 'You shall know the truth and the truth will set you free'. Jesus was not talking about our perception of the truth, but the truth itself. It's only when you see things as they really are that you can be free.

This is in fact what Neo discovers in *The Matrix*. There is reality and there's your perception of reality.

Clip Two: The Desert of the Real

Neo takes the red pill and boards the Nebuchadnezzar. Morpheus introduces him to his crew.

Morpheus now shows Neo what the world really looks like, without the illusion created by the Matrix.

Morpheus shows Neo the world that he knows, the world of the late twentieth century, an urban landscape of skyscrapers and busy people. Morpheus explains that this is a computer simulation – it is a dream world.

He then shows Neo what the world truly looks like, not what is presented to Neo's senses by the Matrix. An American city lies devastated under a sea of ash. There is literally nothing left. Morpheus calls it 'the desert of the real'.

He then relates how all this came about. Mankind, in the early twenty-first century, was united in celebration, marvelling at the magnificent achievement of giving birth to AI (Artificial Intelligence). A singular consciousness spawned an entire race of machines. War broke out. The machines won, and started to use the bio-electric energy of human bodies. Today, Morpheus continues, there are endless fields of human bodies (no longer born, but grown) being harvested for human energy. People live in pods, unconscious that their bodies are being abused in this way, living in a dream world, unaware that they are not free. '*The Matrix*,' says Morpheus, 'is a computer-generated dream world built to keep us under control in order to change a human being into this'. Morpheus shows Neo a battery. Neo resists. Morpheus concludes, 'I didn't say it would be easy, Neo. I only said it would be the truth'.

What is the truth?

According to the Bible, in the beginning God created the heavens and the earth. Human beings lived in perfect harmony with God and each other. Then the devil entered the garden, tempted Adam and Eve to disobey God, and since that day, the cosmos has been under the dominion of evil. Human beings have not been free. Rather, they have become slaves to sin. We live in denial about this. We choose to live in a dream world of consumerism. But this never satisfies the deep longings of the soul. We long for the truth. We long for liberation. The cry of freedom rises up from within our hearts.

Clip Three: Death and Resurrection

Back to *The Matrix*. Morpheus and the crew have been searching for the One who will set them free from the tyranny of the Matrix. They believe Neo is the person who will do this. Neo is the Messiah figure in *The Matrix*.

How then does freedom come to the slaves of the Matrix?

Two hours into the film, Neo is trying to exit the Matrix and return to his real body on board the *Nebuchadnezzar*. He is running towards a ringing telephone – the means by which he and his crew re-enter the ship. But three Matrix agents are on to him and what's worse, the *Nebuchadnezzar* is under attack too.

Neo finds his way to the ringing phone only to find Agent Smith waiting there. The agent points his pistol at Neo's chest and fires. Neo falls to the ground. The agent empties his cartridge into Neo's body as the phone continues to ring. Back on board the ship, Morpheus and Trinity are dumbstruck as Neo's vital signs register his death. 'It can't be', Morpheus declares.

Back at Neo's corpse the agents realise, he's dead. Agent Smith bids him farewell. Then we are back on board the ship again. Trinity is leaning over Neo's body. She tells him that she loves him and kisses him on the lips. 'You can't be dead, because I love you. You hear me? I love you'.

In a neat reversal of *Sleeping Beauty*, Neo awakens as he is kissed. Back in the Matrix, he stands up. The agents fire at him, but Neo manages to freeze the bullets in mid flight and they fall to the ground. As the music builds to a crescendo, Morpheus says, 'He is the one'.

Agent Smith charges at Neo, but he is no match for the reborn Neo and he is killed, light pouring out of his body after Neo has dived through him. The other agents run in terror. Neo returns to the *Nebuchad- nezzar*. The attack lifts and he embraces Trinity once again.

The film ends with 'system failure' registered on the central computer programme of the Matrix.

The Offer of Freedom

In *The Matrix*, freedom becomes a possibility through the death and resurrection of Neo Anderson. But *The Matrix* is fiction, not fact. What happened to Jesus of Nazareth is fact, not fiction. Jesus died on a cross outside the walls of Jerusalem in about AD 33. He himself said that he was the 'Son of Man' and that he was going to give his life 'as a ransom for many'. The blood that he shed at Calvary was the price paid that we might be redeemed, set free from our slavery to sin.

But the events of Good Friday were not the end of the story. On the following Sunday, in the early hours of the morning, God raised Jesus from death. The resurrection of Jesus is the most critical moment in human history. Hundreds of people met the resurrected Jesus in the fifty days between his resurrection and his return to his Father beyond space-time. Jesus had conquered the powers of darkness through his sacrificial death and his supernatural resurrection. Through these momentous events, the devil's hold over the earth has been destroyed. Human beings can be freed from sin to know God and live life in all its fullness – we can experience the kiss of the Trinity.

The saddest scene in the movie involves a man called Cypher, the Judas figure in the film. He is the one who betrays Morpheus and his band. During the scene in question, Cypher re-enters the Matrix (without his friends' knowledge) and has a meal with Agent Smith. Cypher is eating steak and drinking red wine. He knows they are not real, but he would rather live as a slave than as a free person. As he puts it, 'After nine years, you know what I realise? Ignorance is bliss'. So, he asks that once he has betrayed his friends he would be re-introduced to the Matrix as a wealthy person so that he can live in a dream world rather than the real world. 'I want to remember nothing', he says.

If you want it, the truth will set you free – it's your decision. As someone has said, 'You are free to choose, but the choices you make today will determine what you will have, be, and do in the tomorrows of your life.'

I feel a little like Morpheus (though not as well dressed!). I am holding out a red pill and a blue pill. It's your choice. As Morpheus says to Neo, 'I can only show you the door. *You* have to walk through it. . . .'

THE BIG PICTURE 2

by J. John & Mark Stibbe

Featuring

Minority Report
The Green Mile
Lord of the Rings: The Fellowship of the Ring
What Women Want
Shrek
Unfaithful
Simon Birch
Bridget Jones's Diary

to be published in 2003

Other Titles from J.John and Mark Stibbe

Walking With God

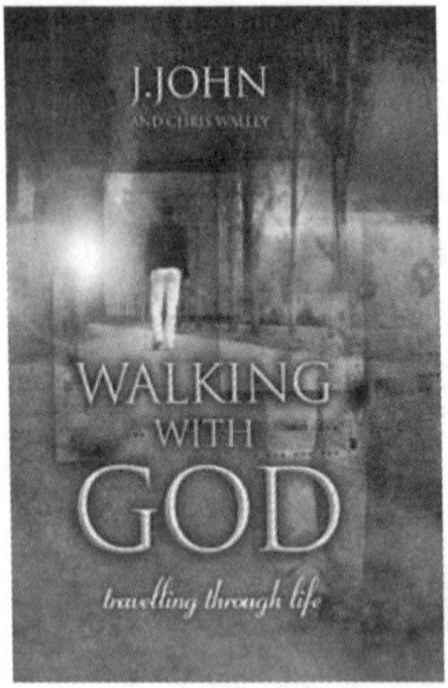

J.John and Chris Walley

Living life is like walking along a path: there are choices to be made and obstacles to face. But there are lots of questions.

- ❑ **How do we find the right way?**
- ❑ **Is there a destination at the end of it all?**
- ❑ **Can anybody help us along the path of life?**

Around 2,750 years ago, a prophet spoke to a society that was asking the same questions. 'What does God want?' he asked and - in the next breath - gave the answer: 'To act justly and to love kindness and to walk humbly with your God.'

In this book, you will find there are answers. There is a right way to walk through life, there is a destination, and there is someone who will walk along the path of life with us.

ISBN: 1-86024-274-X ● Price: £7.99

Marriage Works

J.John

We are constantly being told that marriage is a doomed institution. The prevailing attitude is that you can try marriage if you want - just don't expect it to last. Popular speaker J. John has written *Marriage Works* because he believes that marriage does work and he wants to help you make it work for you. *Marriage Works* is a positive statement that marriage can work and is a helpful and sympathetic guide to the interior of marriage. In this book J. John considers:

- ❑ **what marriage and love are all about**
- ❑ **singleness, the delicate issues of dating, the alterntives to marriage, and the awesome seriousness of making that decision**
- ❑ **creating a marriage: the wedding, the early days, and the principles of making your marriage a success**
- ❑ **defending your marriage: resolving conflicts, affair-proofing, crisis management and marriage repair.**

Whether single or engaged, just married or married for years, happily married or struggling, this book with its thoughtful and witty, down-to-earth wisdom is for you.

ISBN: 1-86024-239-1 ● Price: £7.99

Calling Out

J.John

Calling Out is a serious attempt to provide a practical, all round guide, enabling all believers to share Jesus. Despite its wide-ranging scope, *Calling Out* is written for all Christians, from new believers onwards in a fresh, lively and jargon free style.

A passionate and compelling guide to evangelism by one of its most gifted practitioners covering the following areas:

- ❑ **Why do we need to share our faith?**
- ❑ **What is the message we have to share?**
- ❑ **Why do most of us find it so hard to do?**
- ❑ **How do we answer all those hard questions?**

ISBN: 1-86024-359-2 ● Price: £7.99

Calling Out – The Studies

J.John

Calling Out is a practical, all round guide that shows all believers how they can share their faith in a fresh, lively and jargon-free style. Now, this companion book of Bible studies will to help equip Christians to multiply their faith.

In *Calling Out*, J. John explained what he had learned about evangelism. These seven studies - which follow the order of that book - are designed to help small groups work through some of the lessons that the Bible teaches about calling out effectively with the good news of Jesus Christ.

ISBN: 1-86024-232-4 ● Price: £9.99

A Box of Delights

An A-Z of the funniest, wisest and most poignant stories, proverbs, jokes and one-liners.

Compiled by J. John and Mark Stibbe

ISBN: 1-85424-547-3 • Price: £8.99

A Bucket of Surprises

An A-Z of the wittiest, shrewdest and most memorable stories, proverbs, jokes and sayings.

Compiled by J. John and Mark Stibbe

ISBN: 1-85424-588-0 • Price: £8.99

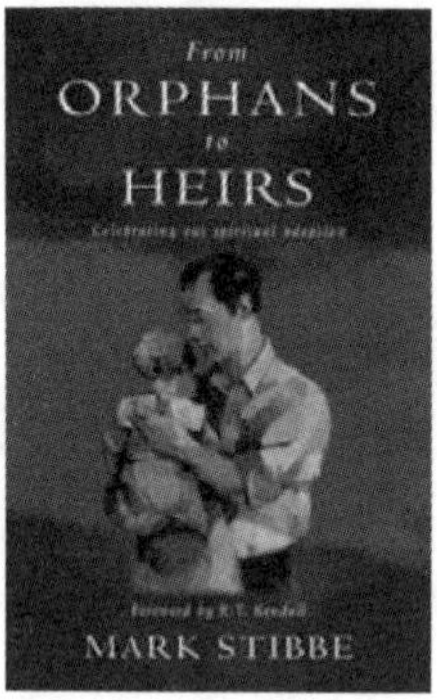

From Orphans to Heirs

Mark Stibbe

An exploration of what being adopted into God's family means. So often, we continue to live as spiritual orphans, forgetting that thanks to the saving work of Jesus we have been made sons and daughters of God. Mark Stibbe explores this image of adoption and shares his own story of growing up as an adopted child and the insights his experiences gave him into the heart of God. He shows how we can experience God's fatherly love, through the work of the Holy Spirit.

ISBN: 1-8410-1023-5 • Price: £6.99